THE CONDEMNED

David Jack Bell

FIRST EDITION

DELIRIUM BOOKS
P.O. Box 338
North Webster, IN 46555
srstaley@deliriumbooks.com
www.deliriumbooks.com

Copy Editor: David Marty

ACKNOWLEDGEMENTS

Special thanks go to Greg F. Gifune, a remarkable editor whose faith in my work has made all the difference. I'd also like to thank Shane Ryan Staley, Dave Kendall and everyone at Delirium for making this happen. Thanks to Molly for taking the manuscript to the beach and answering all of my questions. Some great teachers have helped me along the way: Tom and Elizabeth Monteleone, F. Paul Wilson, David Morrell, Brian Keene, Brock Clarke, Eric Goodman, "Crazy" Jim Reiss, and everyone at the Borderlands Boot Camps. Finally, thanks to my friends and family, especially Mike and Penny McCaffrey and my parents, Herbert and Catherine Bell.

For Molly, who always believed

And in memory of Andy Radcliffe (1975-2002)

The lights are much brighter there.
You can forget all your troubles,
forget all your cares.
So go downtown,
things'll be great when you're
Downtown
no finer place for sure
Downtown
everything's waiting for you.

~ Petula Clark

Praise for
David Jack Bell's
The Condemned

"David Jack Bell's *The Condemned* is an exciting, fast-paced novel with a highly original spin on the zombie mythos. As thought-provoking, moving, and socially relevant as it is brutal and horrifying, *The Condemned* is a remarkable first novel that will undoubtedly secure Bell's position as an electrifying new voice in the genre."

—Greg F. Gifune, author of *Dominion*

"David Jack Bell creates characters you care about and he tells you stories you've never heard before. Watch out. This guy's going to be one of our best."

—Thomas F. Monteleone,
Bram Stoker Award Winning author of
Fearful Symmetries and *Blood of the Lamb*

"*The Condemned* gave me the tingle I felt when I read Richard Matheson's *I Am Legend* for the first time. This is a wonderful, forceful, moody book that's as palpable as it's engaging. Pay attention to David Jack Bell. This is the start of an impressive career."

—David Morrell

"David Jack Bell writes with freshness and immediacy, and I look forward to following his bright arc across the horror heavens."

—Scott Nicholson

"David Bell is the real deal, a true storyteller with a style as compelling as a news bulletin. You just keep turning the pages."

—Ed Gorman

"If David Goodis or Jim Thompson had written a zombie novel it might have been something like this. It comes complete with a sly social commentary as well. Bell's is an impressive debut..."

—Jack Ketchum

"In *The Condemned*, David Jack Bell has created a beautifully written and compelling novel, filled with fascinating characters, and turning on a unique storyline that may just make it a classic, in time."

—T.M. Wright, author of
A Manhattan Ghost Story and *I Am the Bird*

ONE

The sound of shattering glass, a window breaking nearby in the house, brought me out of a deep, troubled sleep.

The baby's room, I thought. Someone's in the baby's room.

I threw the covers back and moved cautiously down the hallway. The house was cold, causing the skin on my bare arms and legs to break out in gooseflesh. I stopped outside my daughter's room and listened.

The night was quiet, the only sound the rush of blood in my ears.

I looked through the door, into the baby's room. In the indistinct light, I saw a figure standing at my daughter's crib, its back to me. I didn't speak, didn't scream. Something about the figure's posture — his gray work clothes, his hair — looked familiar, almost comforting. I hesitated. The shattered window gaped, the night wind fluttering the white curtains in the dark like a hovering ghost.

Finally, I stepped into the room.

The man at the crib slowly turned, revealing his face.

"Vince," I said. "How...How did you get back?"

Vince didn't respond, and I saw this was not the Vince I once knew, my work partner and best friend. This Vince had sallow, sunken cheeks, and his eyes looked back at me with a complete absence of recognition. They were lifeless and empty, *like the blank eyes of a dead fish.*

The wind picked up, fluttering the curtains higher, and bringing to my nostrils an odor of decay, like rotting meat. It came from Vince, leaked out of his pores. I breathed through my mouth to keep from gagging.

"That's my baby girl you've got there," I said, indicating the tiny bundle in Vince's arms. He had taken her from the crib, and she lay in his grasp in the quiet room, seemingly at ease with the night's disruptions. "She hasn't done anything to you."

Vince shifted the baby in his arms, lifting her a little higher.

"Why don't you just let me take her?" I said. "You can do whatever you want to me, but don't hurt Sophie. She's not involved in any of this..."

Vince shook his head, but the movement was more than simple refusal. It was defiance. He opened his mouth and showed his teeth the way a feral animal might warn off a threat to his food supply.

"Vince, please..." I tried to move forward, to lunge for my daughter and save her life. But I couldn't move. Rooted in place, my body refused to cooperate, and like a man stuck in concrete, I helplessly watched the nightmare unfold before my eyes. "Don't!"

Vince's grimace turned to a triumphant smile.

Teeth still bared, he bent to my child's throat, and began to feed...

*   *   *

I sat bolt upright in bed.

After days of lousy sleep, my nerves were frayed and jangling like a live wire. The clock on the bedside table read 6:27, three minutes before the alarm would ring. My legs were tangled in the sheets, binding my feet together in something like a burial shroud. I kicked and pulled at them, mostly freeing myself.

"Jesus."

I rubbed my eyes with the palms of my hands, creating red and green starburst patterns on my retinas, but they didn't replace the images I'd seen through the night. On those rare occasions when I managed to sleep, the nightmares came. For thirteen days straight, the same thing: I'd find myself back in the city, back among the dilapidated, empty buildings, the broken glass, the smell of urine…and Vince, always Vince, reaching out for me, calling my name. And me, frozen in place, unable to move, unable to speak, unable to help, even though I knew I had to. But now I'd dreamed of something new: our home being breeched, Vince in our daughter's room, Sophie in danger. And still, I did nothing, could *do* nothing but stand there and watch helplessly.

I reached over to the other side of the bed. "Nicole?" I whispered. Her side of the bed was empty and cold, her half of the covers thrown aside. "Nicole?" I said, louder.

She never woke up before me unless the baby cried. And I'd have heard the baby crying. I dug out from under the sheets and staggered into the hallway. The door to Sophie's room was open, the light on. Nauseous and scared, a hollow pit grew in the center of my gut like someone had scooped my core out.

I went into the baby's room and over to the crib. Empty. Just the yellow blanket and the silly stuffed ducky that Sophie slept with.

I darted back to the hall and stopped, the carpet soft beneath my bare feet and the back of my T-shirt damp from night sweats.

From the kitchen, noises. Dishes clattering, and then, faintly, the sound of Sophie's chattering. Nonsense syllables repeated over and over again. I moved to the end of the hall and looked in the kitchen. Nicole stood at the sink, her back to me. Sophie, lost in her own world, sat in her high chair, playing with her spoon. The bright overhead light illuminated their simple morning routines.

Behind me, the alarm clock kicked in, an insistent, annoying bleat, a call to begin the day. It sounded more like a warning. I went and turned it off.

The first ordinary day of what I would come to call the rest of my life had begun.

*   *   *

"You're really going to do this, aren't you?"

Nicole stood at our kitchen counter, the sleeves of her bathrobe pushed up past her elbows. Her eyes were puffy from sleep, and her hair went in about twenty different directions. But her eyes bore in on me, nearly pinning me to the wall.

"It looks that way, doesn't it?" I said.

She turned away, back to the dishes that had piled up in our sink. Her silence was like a slap in the face, and when Sophie started banging her spoon against the tray of her high chair, I welcomed the distraction.

"Hi, Sophie girl," I said. "Hi, baby."

"Da-da. Da-da. Da-da."

She started scattering Cheerios everywhere, her arm movements jerky and haphazard.

I sat down at the table. Nicole banged a few dishes around in the sink. It sounded like she was overhauling a transmission.

"I gave the last of the milk to the baby," she said. She offered no apology, made no mention of anything else to eat or drink.

"That's okay," I said. "I probably couldn't eat anyway."

"How did you sleep last night?" Nicole said.

I shrugged. "Okay."

"For someone who sleeps okay, you thrash around a lot." She dried her hands on a dish towel decorated with giant strawberries, a wedding present from some forgotten relative. "You woke me up twice, either mumbling in your sleep or moving around."

"Sorry about that."

The TV played in the corner of our kitchen. The morning news anchor said something about troop movements in Asia then read the latest body count. I didn't hear the number. There were a lot of things I'd learned to ignore. That was one of them.

Nicole tossed the towel away and looked at me. Her eyes showed concern. "Are you sure you're okay?" she said.

"I'll be fine when I'm back at work today."

I started feeding Sophie Cheerios. She gummed them like an old man, her eyes as wide as dinner plates.

Nicole came over and scooped her out of the high chair. Sophie made a little noise that indicated surprise.

"She needs her bath now," she said. "I didn't do it last night." Nicole stopped across the room. Sophie grabbed a fistful of Nicole's tangled hair and twisted it in her little hand. Nicole shifted, moved the baby higher on her hip. "You don't have to do this, Jett," she said. "I've done everything but beg, but I'll beg if it'll make a difference."

I considered this woman I had loved for five years. She had given me everything and asked for so little. If I could only just bend in her direction for a change, give something back...but I couldn't. Not about work. "It won't make a difference," I said.

Nicole bit her lip. Time hadn't touched her, and motherhood had only made her more beautiful. She was strong, stronger than me. She wasn't going to cry. She shifted the baby's weight again. "Say bye-bye to Daddy," she said.

Sophie looked at me. She opened and closed her fist, the eleven-month-old version of a wave. Then Nicole turned and they went down the hall and out of sight, leaving me at the table with my thoughts and my stubbornness. "Nicole," I called after them. I didn't know if she could hear me, so I raised my voice in the quiet morning. "Make sure you lock the doors today. Lock all the doors. Please?"

I'd like to say I was doing it all for them—returning to work, trying to protect them—but there was so much more to it than that.

So much more.

* * *

I worked for the city. Never mind which one. By that point, they were all pretty much starting to look the same—like the remains of a once great civilization. And I often wondered what future archeologists would find when they dug us up. No pyramids, no pharaohs. No aqueducts or abacuses, just steel and glass and garbage. Lots and lots of garbage.

I used to say I worked for a dying city, but that was too generous. My city was already dead. It belched out its last productive breath back during the Industrial Revolution, back when we made things besides bombs and planes and tanks. We made those too—don't get me wrong—but only when we needed them, only in times of crisis. Eventually it became a way of life, the only way we knew how to survive.

And who was I to judge anyone? I was a creature of habit like everybody else.

I punched the clock like a rat in a maze, then waited for my piece of cheese.

*   *   *

We worked out of a wrecking yard on the west side of town, about ten minutes from where I grew up and went to grade school. The wrecking yard hadn't always been there. When I was a kid, there was a hospital. St George's, named after a guy who killed dragons. We could sure have used his help.

I parked in the employee lot, turned the car off and waited. It was a beautiful day. The skies were clear, the sun bright. Up above was the promise of warmer weather, the hope for new life springing from the old.

But down below, on the ground where we all walked, the sun reflected off twisted chrome and broken glass. The compacter ran both day and night, sending thick black smoke to the sky, covering the sun in a black scrim and filling our lungs with choking diesel.

I didn't mind going back and doing the work. I could do the work better than anybody alive. I feared the pity, the pathetic looks. The head-shaking and whispers behind my back. I didn't want to be anybody's charity case, the guy whose partner and best friend died in the line of duty.

But like I said, I'm a creature of habit. What else was I going to do with my life? What else could I do? And didn't I owe it to Vince to soldier on, to go back to work and keep doing what we were so good at?

So I willed myself out of the car, and I walked toward the shed with my head down, hoping no one saw me or talked to me. And that became my strategy for that first day: head down, keep moving and don't look back.

*   *   *

We called it the shed, but that word wasn't really right.

We operated out of a cinder-block warehouse large enough to house twenty wreckers, a dispatch center and an office for our supervisor, Ned. It was all city property now, but when I was a kid, there were houses there and trees and wide streets kids used to ride their bikes and play ball on.

I went inside and smelled the familiar odors of oil and rubber. On the far side of the shed, mechanics tinkered with the rigs, and they didn't notice me. I clung to the false and silly hope that I could slink through the entire day without seeing another soul.

I moved to my left, toward our small break room and the time clock where I had to punch in. My false hope died there. When I walked in I saw about ten of my co-workers, smoking cigarettes and drinking coffee. The room turned silent as a grave when they saw my face. It felt almost as bad as one of my nightmares.

I waited for someone to say something, and when they didn't, I went to the clock, found my card and punched it. When I turned back around, the faces still stared at me.

We weren't soldiers or cops or firemen. We didn't have a long tradition or honor codes to draw upon. But no one had ever died in our line of work, and while everyone said the right things at Vince's funeral, I didn't know how they'd respond to me today, when I came back to work and tried to be one of them again.

Bobby Crawford stepped toward me. A big guy with a walrus mustache and knuckles the size of walnuts, he never said much to me. He never said much to anybody. But he was respected. Well respected. And if he told me to walk, I'd walk. "Jett," he said. He nodded at me.

"Bobby."

He studied me for a moment like he didn't know what to do. At first I thought he was pissed, but it took me that moment to realize that the guy just didn't know what to say to me. He stuck out his meaty right hand and nodded at me again. I reached out and shook it, his big hand swallowing mine and grinding my knuckles together. "Welcome back," he said. Then he pulled me toward him a little and gave me a clap on the shoulder with his other hand. It nearly knocked the wind out of me, but I didn't mind. Then the other guys were all around me, and I shook so many hands I felt like I was running for office.

And for a moment, I forgot everything that had gone before, the nightmares and the fear. For a long moment, the burden lifted.

I was back.

*   *   *

After all that, I went to see Ned.

He had a small cluttered office with windows that allowed him to sit at his desk and watch what went on in the garage. When he saw me at the door, he stood up. "Jett. Hey. Well, look who's here."

Ned was at least a hundred pounds overweight, and his skin was bleached out and pale. He looked like he was made of dough. His hair was almost gone on the top of his head, but he combed it over the bald spot in a vain and failed attempt to fool people. When I shook his hand, his grip was limp and cold, like holding a wet washcloth.

"I just wanted to check in," I said.

"Yeah. Sure. Have a seat." He pointed to a chair and we both sat down. I could tell Ned didn't know what to say to me. He had caution etched onto his face, a look that said he thought I was going to jump up and bite him. Ned was a bureaucrat through and through, a pencil-pusher and a by-the-book city employee. He didn't know how to deal with a real live human being. "I'm glad you're back," he said.

"I'm glad to be back."

He nodded. "Nicole okay? The baby?"

"Good. Good."

He picked up a paperclip and started bending it out of shape. He kept his eyes on the clip when he spoke next. "You know, you can take more time if you want it. City regs allow you more time."

"I figured you'd need me."

He dropped the paperclip. "I do, I do. Absolutely." He ran his hand across his forehead. "We're way behind here. Demand for scrap is up, and we haven't been able to get enough. Guys are scared to go out there since...since you and Vince ran into that trouble."

Calling Vince's death "trouble" struck me as the understatement of the century. But I let it go.

"I'm here to do my job again," I said.

Now Ned smiled. I imagined that the little chart in his mind, the one that tracked our actual production versus our goals, started ticking in the direction he wanted it to go. "You're the best, you know that. You were always the best." When Ned smiled, a dimple appeared in his fat cheek. "I think it will be good for morale to see you back. I think the guys are really going to get a lift from this. Most of them."

"Most of them?"

"You know..."

"McGruder," I said.

Ned nodded. "You know how he is. He's difficult."

"He's a prick."

"But you don't have to worry about him. Just ignore

him. You won't have to go anywhere near him."

"About that," I said. "I wanted to ask you a favor."

The good cheer drained from Ned's face. There was no word a bureaucrat hated to hear more than *favor*. "What do you want?" He looked stricken, like I had a gun pressed against his temple.

"I want to work alone," I said.

Ned started shaking his head before I had even finished my sentence. "No, no way." His head kept shaking, and the little flap of skin beneath his chin shook along with it. "No can do. Nobody goes out alone anymore. Nobody. Not after what happened out there to you guys."

"Orders are up, but we can't work alone," I said. "That doesn't make sense."

"I know, I know." He took another swipe at his forehead. "But what can I do about it? My hands are tied."

"You can make an exception for me," I said. "You said I'm the best. Let me go out alone. I can do the work of two guys."

Ned started the head shake routine all over again. "I can't. They want guys working in teams for protection. That way there's always somebody watching for trouble."

I sighed. "So who are you sending me out with?" I said. "I should get some say in who it is."

"I've already got somebody in mind," Ned said. "He's a new guy."

"A new guy?"

"He's good. He's real good." Ned pushed himself out of his chair. "Let me introduce you to him. And I'll tell you all about it on the way."

*   *   *

We were only a few steps outside of Ned's office when McGruder stepped in front of us. "The great man's back," he said.

"Bill," Ned said. "Ease up."

"It's okay," I said. "I don't mind hearing from William."

I hated to admit it, but McGruder was one of the best drivers we had. Ned said I was the best, and maybe I was, but McGruder was as good as me, and on certain days he was better. That made it tough for me to like him under the best of circumstances. But he was also one of the most unpleasant human beings I had ever known, and if he wasn't so good at his job, he would have been run off a long time ago. I also knew that he hated to be called William, so I called him that every chance I got.

"I was beginning to think you were finished here," McGruder said. He shaved his head and wore a leather jacket over the top of his city issued coveralls. "It was kind of nice not having you around."

"Bill," Ned said. "Jett's back. We need him. There's no way we can make our goals without him."

When it came right down to it, I really didn't have the spirit to do a lot of verbal jousting with McGruder. It felt pointless and empty, and more of my life than I liked to admit felt pointless and empty. I started past him, hoping to get on with what Ned wanted me to do.

But McGruder took hold of my arm and stopped me. He leaned in close so that only I could hear him. "I can't believe you can even show your face here," he said.

His breath smelled like coffee and onions.

"William," I said. "I'm not sure I can believe it either."

He looked surprised by my words and so couldn't

think of anything to say back to me. I took the opportunity to free my arm and walk away, with Ned huffing to catch up.

TWO

Ned led me across the garage in the direction of three guys I didn't recognize. While we walked, he told me about my new partner.

"The City's got a new program," he said. "They want to give veterans a chance to get work when they come back…from over there. Since we have so much work and need so many guys, they sent a few of them over to us. That's a good idea, right?"

"Sure," I said. "We should try to help the veterans."

"Exactly," Ned said. He moved with a stiff-kneed gait that made him bounce up and down a little bit. "And these guys still want to help out, you know? They want to serve, they just need to find a way to be able to do it."

"You mean because their hitch is up?"

"Yeah. Right."

I reached out for Ned's arm, and we stopped walking.

"What is it, Ned?"

"What?"

"There's something you're not telling me."

"Now hold it, Jett. That's not fair."

But his eyes started shifting back and forth, refusing to settle on a fixed point. He licked his lips.

I looked over at the three guys who were having their own conversation, talking and laughing and not paying any attention to us yet. They looked like regular guys. A little scruffy, a little ragged, but that was par for the course in our job. But I knew Ned was hiding something.

I moved in close to Ned and spoke in a low voice. I wasn't the biggest guy in the world, but I was a little over six feet tall and broad in the shoulders. With a milquetoast like Ned, it was more than enough to intimidate.

"You're not going to send me back out there with some flake," I said. "Now level with me, Ned. What's wrong with these guys? Are they crazy? Are they nut jobs?"

Ned held his hands up in a placating gesture. It almost looked like he was surrendering to me.

"Take it easy, Jett." He lowered his hands and leaned in. "They were wounded and sent back home. Now they're working for us."

"Wounded? How bad were they wounded? We can't have a wounded man out there, slowing things down." I shook my head. "Come on, Ned. Send me out alone. Don't set me up with a guy like this."

"Leave it, Jett," he said. "You're not going out alone. But I've got you lined up with the best guy in this group. He's been in combat for Christ's sake. Doesn't that qualify him to help you? A combat veteran? Shouldn't that be good enough for you?"

If Ned intended to make me feel guilty, it worked. Like I said, I hadn't been thinking of the war much. Nobody had. But maybe if I could help a veteran learn a new job and get back on his feet, I'd be doing my part. Maybe it would be one one-thousandth of my penance.

I nodded. "Okay, Ned. I'll work with him."

Ned gave me a big smile. "Great. I'll introduce you."

The Condemned

*   *   *

The first thing that struck me about him when he turned around was his age. He really was a kid. Ned introduced me and told me his name, but from that moment on, I thought of him and called him "The Kid." That's who he was to me.

He stuck out his hand, and when we shook, he placed his other hand on top and locked his eyes on mine.

"Jett," he said. "It's a real pleasure, a real pleasure."

He couldn't have been more than twenty years old. He was shorter than me and lean, so lean that his city issued coveralls hung on him like a parachute. He didn't look like he had ever shaved in his life, and sincerity and earnestness oozed out of his every pore. But there was something about the way his grip lingered on mine, and the way his eyes squinted ever so slightly, almost imperceptibly, as they bored into mine, that sent a shiver of unease through me.

"I sure do appreciate you taking me on like this," he said. "I've heard so much about you from Ned and the other guys. I know I'm learning from the best."

I looked around. The other two new guys sort of shuffled their feet and looked at the floor. Ned was beaming like a proud father. The Kid still had me in his grip, waiting for me to say something.

"I'll make you president of my fan club."

The Kid laughed like he had never heard a funnier joke, and then Ned joined in, making strange snorting sounds that I assumed were laughter. When Ned finished laughing, he wiped at the corners of his eyes.

"I knew you two would hit it off," he said. "I knew you'd be perfect for each other."

*   *   *

Since it was my first day back and the Kid's first official day on the job, Ned told us to take it easy.

"Don't overdo it," he said. "Just show him the ropes and get back in the swing of things."

For once, I thought Ned had the right idea. I was glad to be back, glad to have a whiff of my normal life. No sense in taking on too much.

"Okay," I said to the Kid. "Let's get rolling."

"Jett," Ned said. He had that sheepish, scared look again. "Since you were out for awhile..."

"Yeah?" I said.

"Someone else has been using your rig."

"Someone else? Who—" But I knew without even asking. "McGruder."

"Best driver gets the best rig," Ned said. "And you were gone."

"That's fine. Which one do I get?"

"Well, number nine's available."

"Nine? That piece of shit?"

Ned just shrugged, a gesture meant to convey that he didn't make the rules, he only lived by them and enforced them.

"That's okay, Jett," the Kid said. He gave me a best buddies slap on the back, but while he spoke, he stared Ned down as if he were our mortal enemy. "You want that number one rig, you'll have it. You'll have it back in no time."

*   *   *

As we walked to the rig, pathetic rig number nine, I noticed something about the Kid. He walked with a noticeable limp. He stepped just fine with his left leg, but when he stepped with his right leg, there was a hitch, a moment of uncertainty, almost as if he didn't quite trust that everything would follow through and work the way he wanted.

I tried not to look too long. I believed in giving a guy his privacy. And he managed to keep up with me just fine as we walked through the shed. He even managed to climb into the cabin of the rig just fine, me on the driver's side and he on the passenger.

I started telling him about the little things I do to get ready for the day. Checking the gas gauge, looking over the map, checking the radio. But the Kid held up his index finger in the space between us.

"Hold it, hold it," he said.

"What?"

"I know what you're really thinking about," he said. "So just go ahead and ask."

I thought about lying, but what was the point?

"You mean your leg," I said. "I'm wondering what happened to your leg."

"Exactly."

"I figured you get asked all the time," I said. "I was trying to be cool about it. But, yeah, I want to know what happened to you."

"That's cool," the Kid said. He reached into his pocket and brought out a stick of gum. "We're going to be partners, right? And we can't keep shit from each other." He unwrapped the gum and popped the stick into his mouth. He started working on it, making loud smacking noises while he chewed.

I thought about Vince. He and I were best friends, and we did sit in the rig and talk about everything. Our lives, our families, our hopes and dreams. I didn't want to know the Kid that well, but he had a point.

"Right," I said. "No bullshitting."

The Kid reached down to the right pant leg of his

24

coverall and pulled it up. First I saw his black combat boot, then a band of white sock. His leg looked as smooth as his face and tanned a darker shade than the Kid's pale complexion. He used his free hand and knocked against his own calf. It made a dull thud, like knocking on a solid block of wood.

"Stepped on a land mine." He said this as casually as someone else might have reported stubbing their toe. "Took off everything below the knee."

"Jesus."

"I almost bought it," he said. "They had to hit me with the paddles three times. Shocked my ass back to life." The Kid looked wistful as he described the experience, as if he were remembering a rare moment of perfect contentment. "Two weeks in a crappy hospital over there. Two weeks in Germany. Then, five months in the VA learning to walk again." An edge appeared in his voice. "You do *not* want to spend time in one of those places, my friend. It's like a nursing home for young people." He kept up his work on the gum. "I wanted to go back when I could walk again. I begged them to let me go, especially since we're so short of men. No dice. So I figured this was my way to contribute. My way to keep serving."

"You must have seen some shit over there."

"Oh yeah."

I nodded to show I was impressed.

"You're in the city now. You haven't seen anything like it."

THREE

As we drove the mile from the shed to the entry checkpoint, the Kid drilled me with a series of questions. We passed a number of empty, broken down buildings, ones that were built near the turn of the century, but which had long since been given over to the ravages of time and neglect. When my great-grandparents were growing up, that was the best place to live, a neighborhood that bustled with workers and families and businesses. I often wished that I knew what it looked like back then, when everything was new and clean.

The Kid kept talking and asking. He wanted to know exactly what we did and how we did it.

"Didn't Ned go over all of this with you?" I asked.

"He did. But what does he know. You're the guy in the trenches. You're the expert."

So I laid it all out for him.

The job was simple, really. As simple as could be.

We were at war. It had been that way for as long as I could remember.

To fight a war, we needed raw materials. Metal and aluminum to make planes and bombs and guns. Hotshot pilots in military helicopters flew over the dying core of our city and mapped the locations of the abandoned cars. Our job was to go in and collect them so they could be crushed and melted and turned into other things, the things needed to conduct a war.

Simple, really. As simple as could be.

If I didn't do it, somebody else would. And it paid well enough to feed my family in a time when good work was scarce.

The Kid listened to all of this, nodding impatiently. I got the feeling I wasn't giving him the version of our job that he wanted to hear.

"I know all that," he said. "Ned told me that." I waited for him to go on, and he finally did. "I want you to tell me about the City People."

Number nine chugged and puffed. The gears ground when I shifted, and the clutch slipped beneath my left foot. It was a piece of shit, but the city couldn't afford to replace everything that was broken.

"Why do you ask about them?" I said.

"Shit, you know why. They don't tell us the truth about what goes on in the city. The media, the government. Even Ned. They don't tell us jack. But you've been there, you've seen them up close. If I'm going in there with you, I have a right to know. Don't I? No bullshitting, remember?"

The Kid had a way of talking that made it tough to argue. I steered the rig off to the side of the road and stopped. I didn't want to have to explain this while I was driving.

I paused for a moment, gathering my thoughts. Traffic was non-existent down there. Nothing went in and out of the city's center except for our rigs and army patrols. I could have jumped out and laid down in the middle of the road and been safe.

"I'm not sure I really know what they are," I said. I

looked at the Kid. He nodded, urging me on. "They're not human, not anymore anyway. It's funny that we call them the City People since they're not exactly people. Not like us. But it's not that easy to say. They still look human. Some part of them is still human."

Before he died, Vince used to tell me that we owed the City People something. He used to tell me that they had been dealt a bad hand, and if we turned our back on them now, we would all face the same fate. Vince always thought more about those things than I did. I used to hear him, but I didn't really listen.

The Kid didn't like what I was saying at all. He was shaking his head.

"No, no," he said. "They're not like us. Not now, not ever. Even before that thing happened to their drinking water, they were tearing this city down. Did you used to come down here?"

"When I was a kid. My dad worked down here."

"No, I mean as an adult."

"Sometimes," I said. "But there wasn't much left by then."

"That's right. They destroyed it. I hear people saying we should help them out down here, rebuild the place. Bullshit." He made a dismissive gesture with his hand. "It would just get trashed again. I say the army has the right idea. Put up a perimeter and hunt them down. When they're gone, take the land back. It's our city, not theirs."

"But you wanted to know what they're like up close."

The Kid looked at me like he'd forgotten I was there.

"Oh, yeah," he said. "Whatever."

"I've heard things in there," I said, pointing toward the city center.

The Kid raised an eyebrow. "Heard things?"

"Yeah. We were in there once, Vince and me, and I

swear we heard a baby crying in one of those buildings."

"Bullshit."

"It was an infant, a newborn. Vince and I both had kids. We knew what a newborn's crying sounded like."

"Can't be. The drinking water attack killed the kids first. And the ones who are left can't reproduce. That's why they're dying out."

"I know what I heard," I said. "And I've also heard voices in there. Distant and faint. But I've heard them talking."

The Kid started laughing then, making a yelping noise deep in his throat. He even slapped his knee.

"Now I know you're messing with me." He snorted and kept laughing. "I'm going to make you right, Chief. I got here just in the nick of time." He pointed at the dashboard clock, one of the few things that actually worked on number nine. "We're late for work though, buddy. And I don't want to get in trouble on my first day."

He kept laughing while I steered the rig back onto the road and toward the checkpoint.

"Voices," he said. "And babies. Oh boy. Oh Jesus."

FOUR

The army had the city cordoned off with barbed wire and barricades. They had ten checkpoints spaced out around the perimeter that they moved their patrols through. They also allowed us to go in and collect the cars, during daylight hours only.

We pulled up to checkpoint Orange, the one we needed to enter that day. Ned had assigned each rig an area of the city to work, and I felt certain it was no coincidence he gave us the one closest to base. As much as Ned's meddling and worrying bothered me on most days, his choice to protect me on my first day back gave me a measure of comfort. Just seeing the city in the distance brought back everything from the past, and if the Kid hadn't been sitting next to me, urging me on with his complete confidence in my abilities, I might have turned around and headed right back to the shed. The source of my nightmares lay straight ahead, separated from me by the wire and guns of checkpoint Orange.

Three guys in full battle gear worked the gate. One of them, a sergeant, stepped out with his hand up to stop us.

"Morning," he said. "Got your orders?"

"Sure."

I handed the necessary documents over. The guy looked to be about ten years older than me. I could see some gray hairs around the edge of his helmet. I had heard that they were keeping older guys in longer and longer and sending more and more young guys overseas to fight.

"Nice day, isn't it?" the sergeant said. "Almost makes you forget the world's going in the toilet."

I hoped my name didn't register with him. When Vince died, my name had been all over the news. I didn't want to talk about it, didn't want to be reminded of it. That day lived well enough in my brain. I didn't need others reliving it for me. But he handed the stuff back without any hint that he knew me.

"Thanks," I said.

"Hey, Sarge." The Kid leaned over me and spoke through the open window. "How often do you see these City People?"

The sergeant looked into the cab at the Kid. He pushed his helmet back a little and looked toward the city.

"They keep their distance from us," he said. "They really only come out at night. The daylight bothers them. They're like roaches."

"You ever engage with them?" the Kid said.

"Not often enough for me. But when we do get close to them, we use them for target practice."

The Kid and the sergeant both laughed. I caught a glimpse of the gum in the Kid's mouth and a flash of silver dental work.

"Sounds sweet," the Kid said.

"It is. Pop them in the head. Down they go."

"We really should get to work," I said.

The sergeant looked at me like I had spoiled his fun, but then he nodded.

"Sure thing, guys," he said. "We've got a patrol in there, but call us if you need us."

"Roger," I said.

"And be careful, you hear?" he said. "We've had some trouble in there with you people."

As we drove away, I wished he would have told me that two weeks ago, when I really needed to hear it.

*　　*　　*

We had an order for a pick-up at 13th and Poplar Street. As we drove there, the Kid started talking again, but he seemed to have forgotten all about the City People.

"You're married, right?" he said.

"Sure."

"Kids?"

"A daughter. She's eleven months."

"Damn. A family man."

"What about you?" I said. I had to admit that his questions were helping to distract me from my surroundings.

"What about me?"

"You look too young to be married. Do you have a girlfriend or anything?"

"Nah. I haven't really had a chance since I've been back." He looked out the passenger window. There wasn't much to see. Empty buildings. Vacant lots overgrown with weeds. A school with every window smashed out. "I had a girl when I left, but she moved on when I was in the VA hospital."

"Sorry."

"Fuck her, you know. If somebody can't be true when the chips are down, what good are they?"

I made a right turn, felt the clutch slip. I thought of

Vince's death and my role in it. I didn't say anything. I felt the Kid's eyes on me, like he wanted me to respond.

"Maybe you can find a girl now," I said. "You're young. You're free."

"Shit."

"No, really. You're a war hero."

He looked at me from the corner of his eyes, and I couldn't read the expression on his face at all.

"Is that what you think?" he said.

"Sure. Why not?"

He looked away. "No such thing, brother. There's no such thing."

*   *   *

We rolled up on the car at 13th and Poplar. It was a white Chrysler LeBaron, made sometime in the mid-80s. Rust ate at the edges of the body, and someone had heaved a muffler through the front windshield. The tires were gone. They would have helped with the rubber shortage, but the metal body was our main concern.

I backed the rig into place, lowered the bed. We climbed down. I paused when my boots hit the street. I felt exposed, vulnerable. Even though the morning was cool and clear, the air seemed oppressive and smothering, like the sheets I found myself tangled in at night. When I slipped the keys to the rig into my coverall pocket, my hand shook.

The Kid went right to the back and grabbed the chains. He moved well all things considered.

"Hold up," I said.

"What?"

"Let me do that."

"I know how."

"I know you know." He waited. I didn't want him to

33

think it was because he was injured. And it wasn't. I told him the truth. "I used to do this part with my old partner. Do you mind?"

He handed me the chain. "No sweat."

I crawled underneath the front of the LeBaron, feeling the grit of the street through my coveralls. I attached the chain, then laid back and paused. I almost wished that the Kid would screw something up. Maybe he could pull the lever and let the car run right over my skull, crushing it to pieces. Maybe that would make the world right. But I thought about Sophie and Nicole, and yes, even Vince. There were still things to fight for, things to keep me going.

When I came up, the Kid stared at me.

"You all right, Chief?"

"Right as rain."

"I was worried about you for a second," he said. "Thought maybe you went Section Eight on me."

"Not on a beautiful day like this."

I pulled the lever and the works kicked in. The chain went taut and started dragging the LeBaron up onto the rig's bed. I made small adjustments as it went, the car's bare rims grinding against the metal bed of the rig.

When it was in place, we anchored it down. I turned to the Kid.

"We've got room for one more," I said. "Let's grab the one on 12th."

The work had eased my mind a bit, the routine providing the comfort I had hoped for. I started for the cab, but the Kid didn't move. He was looking around the street, his eyes going over the buildings like he had lost something.

"What is it?" I asked. "What gives?"

"I want to see one," he said.

"See what?"

"A City Person."

I laughed. "You know they only come out at night. Let's get out of here."

He paused a moment, still looking around. Then he climbed into the cab.

*   *   *

At our next stop, we fell to work right away, like a well-oiled machine.

The Kid got the chains, and then I crawled underneath. I fastened everything into place, then came up to finish. I started to tell the Kid that it felt good to be back, good to be working again, but he wasn't there.

"Kid? Hey?"

I thought maybe he went back in the cab, but he wasn't there. And then I hoped that he had just gone on the other side of the rig to take a leak. Nothing.

"Jesus. Goddamn."

I looked in every direction, and there was no sign of him. I simply saw the empty, vacant buildings, the quiet streets. He had gone in search of City People.

I went back to the rig and pulled the lever. Maybe I could just finish with the car, and the Kid would come back. Maybe he hadn't gone far.

Even as I thought it, I knew it wasn't going to happen. I was going to have to go find him, the jackass.

When the car was on the bed, and the bed raised into position, I called the Kid's name. I yelled as loud as I could. The only answer was the sound of my own voice echoing off the brick fronts of the buildings. "I should just leave him," I said. "Let him find his own fucking way out."

But of course I couldn't do that. More than anyone else, I couldn't, and he knew it.

So I started driving, slowly, down the block we were on. I looked both ways, at every building, and blew the horn, hoping that would let the Kid know it was time to go.

I didn't see him in the first block. I figured that he would have turned down the cross street rather than continuing forward down the street we were on. I would have been more likely to see him on the street we were on, but if he turned onto the side street, he would have been out of sight right away.

I went one block on the side street, then two. Nothing.

My palms were slick on the steering wheel, and my heart started to thump until it hurt. I couldn't believe it was happening again. Would I forever be known as the guy who lost partners? Would that be my epitaph? Would my life become a series of failures, an endless loop of letdowns and fuckups that would forever haunt my dreams?

Then I saw something move a block ahead of me. There was a liquor store, Hi-Lo Liquors, and I saw something in the doorway, something that looked to be the color of the Kid's coveralls. I floored it, which didn't do much good in old number nine and carrying a full load at that, but it felt good to be moving with such a clear purpose. I stopped in front of the store and hit the horn three more times.

"Kid!" I yelled through the open passenger window. "Hey, Kid!"

I jumped down from the cab and went to the door of the liquor store. This time I didn't have time to worry about being exposed. I just moved ahead, fueled by fear and adrenaline.

I didn't see anything. No sign of the Kid. Nothing. But the door was open. Its glass was smashed out. All the windows across the front of the store were smashed, and the door hung wide open. I couldn't see much beyond the door because the power was out and the store was dark.

I listened. I thought I heard something rustle.

"Kid?" I waited. "Kid. Get your ass out here. We've got to go."

I looked right and left. Nothing.

"Kid?"

Something rustled again. A scraping, then the sound of broken glass tinkling, like someone was walking over it.

The darkness inside the store resolved into a shape. A human shape. I saw the boots, the city coveralls, then the Kid's face emerging from the darkness.

"Hey, Chief," he said. "What's shaking?"

"What the fuck are you doing, you idiot? Where did you go?"

The Kid didn't seem to mind my anger. He wore a stupid, lopsided grin, and something flashed in his eyes that I didn't recognize.

"Come on back here," he said. "You've got to see this."

"Bullshit. Let's go."

"No bullshit." He jerked his head in the direction of the store. "Come on. There's one back here." His smile grew. "It's just sleeping back there, quiet as a baby." He jerked his head again. "Come on. It's like going to the zoo."

I checked my watch. We should have been heading back. If we came back late, I knew Ned would have a fit. But I'd be lying if I said the Kid hadn't stoked my curiosity. I had seen the City People up close, once. And that was only for a short time in the midst of chaos. To see one now...one that was sleeping.

I turned back to the rig.

"Come on, chief," the Kid said. "Don't turn away."

I opened the door of the cab and reached behind the seat. I found the flashlight first and flicked it on. It still worked. Then I dug around some more and came up with something else. When I turned back around, the Kid was smiling even wider.

"You take the bat," I said. "I'll carry the flashlight."

*   *   *

The flashlight beam cut through the dark, illuminating swirling motes of dust. We saw broken shelves and smashed bottles, the remains of what the residents of this neighborhood used to line up for on payday.

"Where is this thing?" I said.

The Kid was right by my side, so close that our elbows brushed.

"In the back room," he said. "Through that door there."

I stopped. "How do you know that's the only one in here?"

"I looked around."

"It's pitch dark."

"I lit a match. Come on. It's fine."

We shuffled over the broken bottles. I felt the soles of my shoes stick to the floor and hoped it was just spilled and dried liquor beneath my feet. There was an open door in the back wall, one that presumably led into the storeroom. It looked even blacker in there. I aimed the flashlight beam through the opening. It revealed nothing.

"You're nuts," I said. "This is nuts."

"Chief. I ain't going to steer you wrong. Partners, remember?"

I did think the Kid was crazy. But he also gave off a

sense of fearlessness, a confidence that was reassuring in some way. He didn't seem like the kind of guy that something bad could happen to. He'd had his leg blasted off, his heart had stopped, and still he came back. He was practically indestructible.

I moved forward and poked the beam around. Now, I started to see things. Floor to ceiling metal shelves. Boxes marked Jim Beam and Gilbey's and Budweiser. I didn't see anything else.

"Where is it?" I asked.

"Over there."

The Kid guided my hand, pointing the flashlight toward the far left corner of the room. I didn't see anything at first, just shadows and dust. Then I saw a shoe.

I moved the beam up and saw two shoes and legs, and then slowly the entire sleeping form of the City Person was revealed to me.

"Fuck," I said. "Jesus."

"That's right," the Kid said. "There he is. Mr. John Q. Mutant."

It was a man, maybe a few years older than me. He wore a ragged, dirty suit, one that looked like it had been through a war, and he was resting on his side with his hands under his head. It almost made him resemble a sleeping child.

I let the beam linger on his face. The skin looked waxy, the cheeks hollow and sunken. The man was most certainly alive in some sense. His chest rose and fell, but the breathing seemed thready and shallow. But there was a sense of absence hanging over him, the kind I had seen at the few funerals I had attended. Something was missing from this man, and not just because he was asleep in a darkened storeroom. Some aspect of life had been taken from him, leaving a void that surrounded him like an aura.

The Kid moved forward, toward the man and into the flashlight beam.

"What are you doing?" I asked.

"Relax," he said. He stood at the man's feet. "He ain't going to do nothing."

The Kid kicked at the man's feet. The kicks shook the man's body, but he didn't move of his own volition or wake up.

"See that? Dead to the world."

I reached out and took hold of the Kid's sleeve.

"Let's go," I said.

My tug pulled the Kid off balance, and he took an awkward step toward me. I held my hand out to brace him, but he quickly pulled out of my grip.

"I'm fine," he said. He sounded angry.

"We have to go."

When the Kid stumbled, the flashlight beam moved away from the man to a spot on the floor. I angled it back up so that it caught the Kid's face, lighting it from below.

"Bullshit, Chief." He had the bat up and resting on his shoulder, like a baseball player standing in the on-deck circle. "I want to show you something."

"No."

Then something scuffled against the floor in the direction of the man. We both heard it and stopped.

"Move the light," the Kid said.

I swung the beam around. It took a moment for me to fix on the right spot, but when it settled on the man's face, we saw two open eyes, staring up at us.

"Fuck me blind," the Kid said.

My heart froze.

I grabbed his sleeve again and pulled back.

"Let's go."

He shook me off.

"No way. Not now."

He moved forward, and I took a step back. The man on the ground, the City Person, tracked the Kid with his eyes, but otherwise made no move. He looked stunned or slowed in some way, as if his physical movements were a couple of steps behind his brain.

My throat was dry now, but I held the beam as steady as I could on the Kid and the man on the floor. It was like I was watching some horrific stage play, something disturbing and ultimately thrilling that I couldn't turn away from.

"Look at him, Jett," the Kid said. "He sees us. He wants to bite us. Don't you, old boy?" The Kid gave the man a swift, sharp kick in the side. "For all you know, this might be one of them that got your partner." The Kid still had the bat on his shoulder, but then he gripped it with two hands and lifted it, like he was about to take a swing. "A buddy of mine used to come in and hunt these things," he said. "He told me how to do it."

The Kid raised the bat over his head and brought it down, quickly and assuredly, against the man's head. It made a sick thump, the sound of a melon being split open against concrete. I flinched, and the beam moved.

"Little light here, Chief," the Kid said. "I can't see what I'm doing."

I didn't move, but the Kid swung again and again, two more quick blows that made the same noise. The Kid was breathing heavy, and he looked over at me. He smiled, and the flashlight made a crazy light dance in his eye.

"Let's see it," he said.

I moved the beam down. The man's head was caved in, and gray fluid, something the consistency of cream of mushroom soup, oozed through the opening. He wasn't moving, and the Kid's efforts had ended whatever life there was.

"Like a rotten pumpkin," the Kid said. He held the bat out toward me. "Here."

I shook my head.

"Yes. You're not doing it for me. You're doing it for him. Your partner."

His second invocation of Vince got through to me, and the flashlight beam, still directed at the man on the floor, telescoped everything I thought and felt about my partner's death into one fixed point. In that moment, I found a focus for my rage, my regret and my guilt.

I took the bat from the Kid and handed him the flashlight.

As I stepped toward the man, the dead man on the floor, I felt separated from myself, as if I was still watching something play out in front of me rather than being an actor in my own drama.

But when I raised the bat and brought it down, it felt good. It felt right.

So I brought it down again and again, just as the Kid had done, until I felt fluid and tissue spraying back against my face, and then the Kid had me from behind, pinning my arms to my sides and stopping the swinging.

"Easy, Chief. Easy. Take her easy."

I looked at the Kid and he was smiling.

"Save some for next time," he said. "There's plenty more where he came from."

FIVE

Outside, the sunlight hurt my eyes.

I leaned against the side of the rig. My skin felt clammy, and I wiped my face with the sleeve of my coverall. I heard the Kid come up behind me.

"You all right, Chief?"

"What the fuck happened in there?"

The Kid stood on the sidewalk, his hands on his hips. He looked satisfied.

"Revenge," he said. "Pure and simple. Don't it feel good?"

"I feel like shit." I straightened up. "We need to get out of here."

When we got in the cab, the radio crackled. It was Ned checking in.

"Yeah?" I said.

"You okay?" he said.

"Fine. We're coming in."

"I thought you'd be back by now."

"Ned. Lay off."

I hung up on him. I reached for the key, but the Kid's hand landed on mine, stopping me.

"What?"

He let go and leaned back.

"You need me," he said.

"Excuse me?"

"You need me. To help you get better."

"I'll be fine," I said. "It was hot in there."

"I'm not talking about how you feel now. I mean your bigger problem. With your partner."

"It would be a good idea if you didn't mention him again. You didn't know him." I turned the ignition key, and the rig rumbled to life. "In fact, I'm asking for a new partner. I'm done with you. *You're* Section Eight. You're a fucking lunatic. Go hassle somebody else."

"That's fine. Be that way."

"Fine." I dropped the truck into gear, sliding clutch and all.

"But you're never going to feel right, or be right, as long as he's out there."

I still had my foot on the brake.

"Vince is dead," I said. "It's over."

The Kid jerked his thumb toward the liquor store.

"You call that dead in there. He wasn't dead, at least not before you went to work on him with that bat."

"I'm not doing that to Vince. He's gone, and it's time to move on. That's why I'm back at work."

"You'd rather leave him out there, as one of those things, instead of helping him. Instead of really ending it. You need to get to his body and end it."

The Kid wasn't telling me anything I hadn't already thought of. When I couldn't sleep, and therefore enjoyed a temporary reprieve from my dreams, I laid awake, wondering about Vince's exact fate and if there was anything I could do about it. Most of the time, I managed to convince myself that there wasn't anything for me to do. I told myself Vince was dead and gone, and it wasn't worth risking my life—or the lives of others—for someone who was beyond any help I could offer.

When we arrived back at the shed, we unloaded our freight. The Kid and I hadn't talked anymore, and while he jawed with the guys running the crusher, laughing and joking like it was just another day, I went inside and found Ned.

"I want a new partner," I said. "Right away."

Ned looked so relieved to see me that he didn't offer any arguments. He would have given me the moon and the stars if I had asked.

"No problem," he said. "Is something wrong with the gimp? Can't he keep up? It's only lunch time and already the guy can't do the job."

I knew I could have ended the Kid's career with the city right there. Ned would have listened and sent the Kid packing if I told him. But what had the Kid done in that liquor store that I hadn't done? Hadn't we acted the same? And did anyone really need to know that?

"No," I said. "He's fine. He just talks too fucking much."

SIX

Nicole had Sophie on the changing table. I stood in the doorway of Sophie's room, watching this part of our nightly ritual unfold. Nicole moved Sophie around with gentle efficiency, changing her diaper, applying salve to her bottom, pulling on clean pajamas.

"You still haven't said anything about your day," Nicole said. She spoke to me but kept her attention focused on the baby.

"I thought you wouldn't want to hear about it."

"Is that your excuse now?" she said. "You used to tell me you didn't have anything interesting to say. Now you're sparing my feelings."

"Nicole. Let's not start this."

"It's okay," she said. "I'll let it go. I'll assume that your day was as uneventful as mine."

Images from my day hadn't stopped going through my mind. The Kid's face. The man in the storeroom. The bat. They were like a half-remembered dream, something on the border between reality and nightmare. But I knew it was real and true. And I suspected I'd be seeing those images again, in my sleep, a new addition to my brain's catalog of torments.

"They gave me a new partner," I said. "Some guy just back from the war."

Nicole zipped Sophie into her pajamas and turned her head toward me.

"That's interesting."

"Not really. He's sort of an idiot. After we made our morning run, I asked for a new partner."

"How did Ned take that?"

She picked Sophie up and placed her in the crib. We were lucky that Sophie fell asleep fast and stayed asleep. Nicole brushed her hand over Sophie's head, smoothing a stray wisp of hair, and then straightened up.

"He did it," I said. "He gave me a new partner, some guy named Reynolds. He's new, too. It went fine the rest of the day."

"And so you're happy you went back?"

"I'm not sure happy's the right word, but I think it was the right thing. I needed to do it. It was difficult at first, going back into the city, but once we started our routine, I felt..."

"Better?"

"Again, that word might be too strong." I thought for a moment. "I guess I felt...sort of close to normal again. Like I had a purpose."

"Then I'm glad." She turned back around and looked down at Sophie. "Maybe things will get better eventually."

She stood there with her back to me, and I knew that in the early days of our marriage I would have gone to her and slipped my arms around her waist and breathed in the scent of her hair. That seemed like a long time ago, and I couldn't explain the cause of the barrier that now existed between us, the one that prevented me from moving in a way that once was so natural.

"She's a beautiful kid," I said.

"Yes, she is." Nicole cleared her throat. "Jett? I think you should talk to someone about your sleep problems."

"Nicole. Jesus."

She turned from the crib so that she faced me. "They gave you the name of that counselor. Why don't you just call?"

"Because I don't need to," I said. "I'm sleeping better. Like you said, give it time. Right?"

"But they can help you faster. They can speed up the process."

The phone rang in the kitchen.

"I'll get it," I said, welcoming the intrusion.

Nicole shook her head. "Leave it go."

"No."

And I went out to the kitchen and answered.

"Jett…"

It was a woman's voice, low and husky, like the speaker had just woken up. I didn't recognize it.

"Yes?"

"Jett." A pause. An exhalation into the phone. "You went back to work today."

It was a statement not a question.

"Who is —" Then something clicked in my head. "Marie?"

"I don't know how you live with yourself," Vince's widow said. "And I really don't know how you could go back to work." She exhaled again. "But I guess a good thief returns to the scene of the crime."

"How did you know I went back to work today?"

"I have my sources."

I heard children's voices on the other end of the line. Vince's children. He had three. One of the voices rose above the rest.

"Who are you talking to, Mommy?"

"Who am I talking to?" Marie said. "I'm talking to the

48

man who killed your daddy, that's who I'm talking to."

"Marie," I said. But I stopped. I couldn't bring myself to contradict her or argue with her.

Nicole came to the kitchen doorway.

"Marie?" she said.

I nodded.

"Is she drunk?"

"Marie," I said. "I wish I could make this right for you. I wish I could."

She started laughing. "You want to make it right? Are you going to build a time machine and go back to that day in the city? Is that what you're going to do, Jett?"

Her words sounded tinny and brittle coming through the line, like shards of glass entering my ear. Nicole made a slashing gesture with her hand.

"Just hang up," she said. "Hang up."

I shook my head. I couldn't hang up. It was my turn to take the beating, and I intended to hang on the line for every last word of it.

Marie held up her end just fine.

"Are you going to trade your worthless life for my husband's?" she said. "Are you going to bring him back?"

She went on so long, I lost track of time. Nicole walked away, but I stayed, absorbing every word. Every time Marie paused, I cut in with the same thing. It had become my refrain.

"I'll make this up to you, Marie. You and the kids. I swear I will."

*   *   *

After I hung up the phone, I walked through our little house. I checked every door and window in the living room, the kitchen and the garage, making sure they were

49

closed tight and locked. This became my habit in the days after Vince's death, and while the rational side of me knew my nightly lockdown wasn't really needed, a larger part of my mind and soul craved the sense of order and security this habit provided. A small, insignificant gesture, perhaps, but one that remained firmly within my control, and I welcomed that.

With most of the house secure, I let out a deep breath and headed down the hall to Sophie's bedroom. I went in and stood over her crib, looking down at her while she slept. A clown-faced nightlight burned in the corner. The gauzy curtains were drawn, and a soft, white glow spilled through from the street. Sophie made a soft, cooing noise, tightened her grip on her blanket, and continued to sleep.

We had managed, over the previous few weeks, to keep the tensions and events swirling in our household from affecting Sophie. She displayed the typical, simple emotions of an eleven-month-old. She laughed and smiled when we tickled her or played with her. She cried like the world would end whenever she was hungry or needed to be changed. And I hoped that didn't change. I never wanted her to know or understand the kinds of things I had seen in the city—or the things I saw in my dreams. I wanted her to remain untouched.

But Marie's phone call had gotten into my head. Her words swirled in my brain like strong winds coalescing into a larger storm, a tornado of guilt and self-doubt.

I'm talking to the man who killed your daddy.

"I'll make it right for you, too, Sophie," I whispered in the quiet nursery. "I'll make you proud."

Something scratched against the window.

We had a small tree in the side yard, and its shadow showed in relief against the pale curtains. But the tree had been pruned during the winter, and I knew the tips of its branches couldn't reach far enough to scrape against the side of the house.

I took a tentative step in that direction. The wind must have picked up because the shadow of the tree wavered, and then the scratching resumed. It grew louder as I moved closer to the window. I knew that it was something simple, an animal, or perhaps a branch that had shifted or grown back, but my rational knowledge didn't keep a pressure from growing in my chest, a tightening that threatened to restrict my breathing.

The scratching again, louder. More insistent. I took hold of the curtain and pulled it back.

A face. Dark eyes, pale skin. A face staring in at me.

"My God! Vince!" I stumbled back, bracing myself against the crib. "Nicole! Nicole!" I grabbed Sophie and pulled her against my chest. She immediately began to cry as I backed across the room with her, my eyes still trained on the window where I had seen Vince trying to get in at me. When I reached the door, Nicole was there.

"What?" she said. "What?"

"The window," I said. "It's Vince."

"Shhhhh," Nicole said to Sophie. She rubbed her arm. "It's okay, baby. Shhhhh."

"Nic," I said. "The window."

Nicole flipped the overhead light on. "I'll look," she said. "Take it easy. And don't squeeze her so tight."

I loosened my grip on the baby, but kept her pressed against my chest. She was still crying, her face a mask of snot and tears. Having the light on and Nicole in the room relaxed me somewhat, but my entire body shook.

"Let's call the police," I said.

"Just a minute." She sounded irritated.

"Nicole…"

But she went to the window, bent down a little, and pressed her face against the glass.

51

"It's a raccoon," she said. "He climbed up on the ledge." She thumped against the window twice with the bottom of her fist. "He's gone now. Remember, they were in our trash last year?"

"Are you sure?"

"I'm sure." She pulled the curtain closed and came across the room. Sophie's crying had slowed. She was sniffling and taking deep breaths. "Jett, for Christ's sake, it's not Vince, okay? It's nothing to be afraid of."

My heart slowed, but the dull ache remained in my chest. Nicole took hold of my hand with her free one and gave it a squeeze, but I could see the concern in her face. Even Sophie's eyes were wide, looking at me as if she didn't know who I was.

"Okay," I said, still trembling. "Okay. They have faces, you know, raccoons, I must've—"

Nicole nodded. "Of course."

"And I've never heard that scratching before, I thought someone wanted to break in and take the baby, I—"

"I know. Why don't you go out to the kitchen and get some water or something?"

"I'm fine," I said.

"Just go calm down out there," Nicole said. "I'm going to put Sophie back down, and then I'll come out."

Nicole turned away. Her suggestion had been more like a command. I was still shaky and not in any position to put up a fight with anyone. But when I stepped back out into the hallway, I paused. At the end of the hall, the kitchen was dark, and in the opposite direction, so was our bedroom. I had the same feeling there, in my own home, that I had in the city with the Kid. I felt exposed, a sitting duck. I felt vulnerable. And the thought of walking into the darkened kitchen alone suddenly terrified me.

I heard Nicole talking to Sophie behind me. She spoke in comforting tones, her voice a soothing balm to the baby's fears. I willed myself to walk away, to move down the hall and reach my hand into the kitchen. I fumbled for the switch and flicked it, illuminating the kitchen with the harsh fluorescents. I scanned the room. Nothing. Just the chairs and the table, the dishes in the drainer. The refrigerator hummed and snicked off, completing its cycle. But nothing to fear at all. I went to the sink, filled a glass with water and took it to the table.

When I was a kid, I used to get scared like any other kid. I thought monsters lived under my bed, and I feared that murderers would be able to come in my bedroom window at night and hack me to pieces while I slept. On nights when the fears grew too intense for me to even remain in the room, I used to go into the hallway and stand outside the door to my parents' room. They slept with their door open, and I would stand in the darkened hallway of our old house and watch them sleep. Their bodies rose and fell rhythmically, their light snores the only sound in the quiet of the night. I never said a word, and I never woke them. It was as though my voice was frozen and choked off somewhere deep in my throat. Even back then, the notion of asking for help and appearing weak and scared terrified me more than anything I could imagine living under my bed.

I spent many a night in that hallway, sitting on the floor, knees pulled to my chest while watching my parents sleep. Some nights I'd feel myself dozing off, and I'd stumble back to my own bed, able then to finally fall asleep. But other nights, I stayed in the hallway for hours, and only when the edges of the windows began to lighten with the sunrise did I go back to my own room without ever letting on that I hadn't been there the entire night.

Nicole came into the kitchen, her bare feet padding across the floor. She went to the refrigerator and took out a carton of milk. "She's asleep," she said. She carried the milk to the sink and took a clean glass out of the drainer. "She's fine. She's really a good sleeper."

"We're lucky," I said. "I know a lot of kids don't sleep very well."

She filled her glass with milk and remained standing at the sink. "Do you still think you don't need help, honey?"

"Jesus, Nic, I was trying to protect our baby."

"You know it's not that simple. You've never acted like this before."

I took a long swallow from my water.

"How long did you stay on the phone with Marie?" she asked. "What the hell did she say to you this time?"

"Nothing I didn't already know."

"If you want to protect Sophie, you should get help. You scared her tonight." She gazed down into her milk. "And me."

I stood up. "I'm going to sleep. I'm tired."

"I wouldn't think you'd be so eager to do that."

"What do you mean?"

"Considering the dreams you've been having, I wouldn't think you'd be in a hurry to rush off to bed and close your eyes."

"That's real supportive, isn't it?"

"No, it's not. I know it's not. It's really shitty, in fact." She dumped her milk down the sink. "But Marie and I used to be best friends, you know. We used to talk on the phone every day. We shared everything."

"I know."

"Do you?"

"Of course I do. Why would you ask me something like that?"

"Because I want you to remember that you're not the only one who lost some thing the day Vince died. And I don't want to do nothing and end up losing something else."

*　　*　　*

I went in early the next morning and found Ned in his office. He had a doughnut in his hand, and white frosting was smeared across his chin. When he saw me, he smiled.

"Nice work yesterday," he said. "A slow start, but you got right back into the swing of it. I guess the Kid was slowing you down."

"About him."

"I might have to reassign him. Maybe he should work in an office somewhere, filing papers or answering phones."

"I want him back," I said.

"You what?"

"I want the Kid back. I want to partner up with him again."

"You told me to get rid of him yesterday—"

"I know. I changed my mind. I'll work with him again."

A bureaucrat like Ned just couldn't understand somebody changing their mind so fast. He stared at me like he thought I was playing a trick on him.

"You did ask me to get rid of him, didn't you?" he said.

"I did. But I thought about it, and I realized that I should be helping the Kid along, rather than casting him off. I should be mentoring him, you know? Giving him a real chance to learn the job."

Ned gave a hopeless little shrug. "Okay. If you want

him, you've got him. Hell, I put him on with Baker, and Baker comes in here at the end of the day telling me the Kid's a fruitcake. What can I do? The city sends who they send. When he comes in, you can tell him."

"Thanks, Ned."

I was at the door when Ned's voice stopped me.

"Jett?" he said.

I stopped and looked back.

"Are you sure about this? I don't want him slowing you down."

"He won't," I said.

SEVEN

I waited in the parking lot, cooling my heels. Behind me, the crusher went on, monotonously, brainlessly crushing the cars into scrap. I wondered if it even had an off switch, or if there was one, did anybody know how to use it.

The Kid finally came walking up ten minutes later. He had a beaten-up plastic grocery bag in one hand — his lunch, I supposed — and that stupid grin on his face. He didn't look angry. In fact, he looked pleased to see me.

"What are you so happy about?" I said.

"It's a great day to be alive, isn't it?"

"I talked to Ned. You're back on with me today. Permanently."

"Are you sure you want me? I recall you saying I was a lunatic yesterday."

"I think I can use your help."

"Good man, Chief," he said. "You're seeing the light."

"Go clock in," I said. "I'll get the rig started."

"Aye-aye." He saluted me.

I didn't walk away. There was something else I wanted from the Kid.

"When you were over there, in the war, you must

57

have lost some friends. Right?"

The Kid's grin dimmed by a few watts.

"Every day," he said.

"Do you ever hear from their wives or anything?"

"I'm not very good at keeping in touch with people," he said. "Those things tend to fall away from me."

"You might be smart," I said. "All right. I'll see you at the rig. Ned promised me a better one today."

"Saddle up," the Kid said. "Lock and load."

*   *   *

On my way through the garage, I ran into McGruder. He was standing by his rig—*my rig*, as I still thought of it—in his full badass regalia. I planned on walking by without saying anything, but the closer I got to him, the more it bothered me that he was using my truck.

So I opened my mouth.

"Don't get too attached," I said. "I'll be back driving her again soon."

"This?" McGruder pointed at the truck. "I figured this rig would hold too many bad memories for you. Too many reminders of past failures."

"You know what, McGruder? Just stay out of my way."

"That's it?" he said. "That's all you've got?"

"It's all you need to know."

"Then let me tell you what you need to know," he said. He took the sunglasses off, folded them and put them in the pocket of his leather jacket. He stood close enough to me that I saw the stubble where he shaved his head. "It should've been you who died out there. At least Vince thought about other people. He didn't walk around here like his shit didn't stink. And now you come back, the tragic hero, and we're all supposed to feel bad for you and help you out? I'm supposed to give my rig up for you?"

"Keep it."

"I will." He studied me, his eyes drilling into mine. "You should have stayed away. I'm sure Vince's family would be happy if you just left town. Why don't you do the right thing, huh? Quit putting them through this."

"What do you care about his family?" And then something made sense to me, something I had been wondering about since the night before. "You told Marie I was back at work, didn't you?"

"Just do the right thing for them," McGruder said.

I saw the Kid coming my way, moving as fast as he could with his step-hop gait.

"Don't worry," I said. "I am."

*   *   *

The Kid seemed unusually quiet that morning as we loaded up, rolled through the checkpoint and headed toward our first pick up. I expected him to be chipper as a Girl Scout, full of energy for the job we had to do and the unspoken agreement that I would go hunting with him. I was about to ask him what was going on when he pointed to the side of the road.

"Pull over," he said.

"What gives?"

"We need to talk."

I guided the rig to the curb, feeling a little uneasy as I did. Something had shifted between the two of us, and it was starting to look like I was taking orders from the Kid instead of the other way around.

"What's your problem?" I said. "I thought you'd be ready to work."

"You have to come clean," he said. "It's time."

I started to object, but there was no point. I knew what the Kid meant, and I knew that he was right.

"What happened to Vince?" he asked. "It's time to spill the beans."

"I figured you would've heard the story by now. All the talk around the shed and all—"

"Other people's versions don't interest me. I want to hear yours, before we go any further."

"I really don't like to talk about it," I said. "In fact, I haven't actually talked about it with anyone but the authorities."

"All the more reason to tell me," he said. "Remember—no secrets between partners."

I wanted to resist more, but a small part of me felt relieved to be able to tell someone about this. So I took a deep breath and told the Kid the story of Vince's death, a story I had refused to tell to those who most wanted and needed to hear it: Nicole and Marie.

EIGHT

At the end of February, the mayor announced a contest. The team that brought in the most cars during the month of March would receive a five thousand dollar bonus — twenty-five hundred a man. Vince and I had kids and wives and bills. Our house had a leak in the roof, and a hot water heater that worked when it felt like it. Twenty five hundred could go a long way.

And Vince and I really believed we were the best. We knew it. Our production numbers were consistently ahead of our peers. We always brought in the most cars; the most raw pounds of scrap. We figured the twenty-five hundred was ours. And for most of the month it was, as we led the way from the very start.

But near the end of the month, things turned. McGruder and his partner, Danny Priest, started catching up. At first, we didn't notice. They made up a little ground here, a little ground there. But by the last week of the month, they were within striking distance. McGruder started talking smack, telling us we were choking it away, that the money was going to be his.

And the truth is, I was choking. It felt like someone had tied a rope around my neck. And given it a good yank.

The Condemned

I had already spent the twenty-five hundred. I had already called the contractor who had started on the roof. I had already bought the water heater. I figured that with a new baby, I couldn't afford to let things like that slide. I had to provide everything, as best I could. We already had a car payment, a mortgage, credit cards. I didn't want anything else in the pile. One more brick, and the wall might fall on top of me.

But something else was happening to me.

I didn't feel as brave as I used to.

Since Sophie was born, I had felt myself tightening up, playing it safer. Letting Vince do more and more of the risk-taking.

*   *   *

The Kid interrupted my story.

"I never wanted to go on patrol with a guy with a baby under a year old, or a girl back home he just started fucking."

His gum popped a mile a minute, like tiny rifle reports.

"Why?"

"Head in the clouds," the Kid said. "Head in the clouds."

*   *   *

It all came down to the last day of the month, the last day of the contest. March 31st.

We started the day ahead by one, and we knew we had to hump it all day long to keep the lead and win. I'd kept my doubts and worries to myself. I kept everything to myself. But Vince knew better. He was smarter than me.

"What's on your mind, partner?" he said.

"Nothing," I said.

We were at the checkpoint, ready to go in and do our thing. Vince kept looking at me from the driver's seat. He had thick dark hair and dark eyebrows. He wasn't the kind of guy who would let you off the hook.

"Bullshit. What is it?"

My hands rested in my lap, but they were clenched into fists so tight my knuckles ached.

"Nothing," I said. "I just really want to get that twenty five hundred."

"Don't worry about that, partner. I'll bring it home for us."

*　　*　　*

And throughout the course of the day, he did.

We did.

We had one of our best days ever. We found the cars without thinking, and loaded them up without having to speak to each other. We were like machines, moving as quickly and efficiently as our equipment would allow us. We didn't have to say it, but we knew we were going to win. We could feel it.

And I started to feel better as the day went on. I started to feel as though things were going to work out the way I wanted them to. The bills would get paid, the house would get repaired. The life ahead for my little family might improve.

But there was a problem. Late in the day, when we checked our progress against the other drivers, we found out that McGruder had been keeping pace with us all day, leaving open the possibility that he could pass us and get the money for himself.

We only had time for one more run, one more pass

through the city to get what we could and secure the reward.

We found the first car right away. A pick-up, powder blue, with bumper stickers across its back end encouraging us all to give peace a chance and plant a tree.

Too late for that, I thought as we hoisted it into place on the rig.

Vince walked back to where I stood.

"Just got a call on the radio," he said. "Ned authorized an extra hour of work."

"Yeah? Must be the kickbacks he gets from the mayor's office."

"Something like that."

Vince looked up. It was just past six—our normal quitting time—and the sky was starting to change color. The big puffy clouds were turning purple underneath, and a thin band of red had started to seep above the jagged line of rooftops in the distance.

"You want to grab one more," I said. "Even if McGruder stays out, we should be able to take him with one more."

Vince scratched at his chin. He looked like a wise man, pondering life's eternal mysteries.

"I don't know," he said. "I think we've got it now. It's getting late."

A part of me was relieved to hear Vince say that. Everyone treated us as equals and gave us both credit for our success, but when I thought of us, I thought of Vince as the captain and me as the first mate. I trusted his instincts about such things and was willing to follow his lead.

But still, I couldn't let go of the money. When I thought about it, something tightened in my chest, a desire so strong I could almost swear my mouth watered. I wanted the twenty-five hundred. I needed it.

"What if we just took a quick cruise through this block," I said. "If we see something, we'll grab it. If not, we head back."

Vince shook his head. "You're not getting greedy on me, are you partner?"

"Maybe a little." The truck we were working on was in place. I finished securing the chains, gave them a good tug to double check. "You know how it is...kids...bills...a wife."

"You know they'd rather have you than the money," he said.

But he agreed to take a quick look at the streets in our immediate vicinity.

*   *   *

We didn't find anything.

Every time we turned a corner, we found an empty street. Vince kept shaking his head.

"It's not our day," he said.

"One more. Just one more."

We looked for twenty minutes, as the sky turned the color of ink, and the evening star popped into the sky like a beacon calling us home. I was about to give in to Vince's wishes and tell him to get us out when I saw something.

"Wait, wait," I said. "Stop there."

"What?"

"Back up."

Vince put the rig in reverse—it beeped its warning to the empty streets—and brought us even with a wide alley that ran between two buildings on the passenger side.

"There," I said, pointing.

A silver Saturn, nearly new, sat twenty feet back from the opening of the alley, just waiting for us to bring it home.

"That's a five thousand dollar car right there," I said.

Vince looked up at the sky. "I think we should go," he said.

"We've got time." I pointed to the dashboard clock. 6:23. "They don't come out until seven."

"Usually. We've seen them earlier."

I almost gave in. I trusted Vince, respected his good judgment and common sense. But I didn't want to be the guy who always played it safe. I liked being one of the dogs pulling the lead sled. I didn't want to turn into the kind of guy Vince and I made fun of, the ones who had no shot at the five thousand.

I was about to tell him this when he rolled the rig forward ten feet and then threw it into reverse, backing toward the alley in a wide arc.

"Fuck it," he said. "Screw McGruder."

"Yeah."

I beat my fist against the dashboard.

"But we better be damn quick about it," Vince said, looking back, guiding us into place in front of the Saturn.

"We will," I said. "We most certainly will."

Before the rig had even stopped moving, I was out, moving to the back and getting into place. As I lowered the bed, Vince came back and stood beside me. He kept his eyes on the sky.

"Remember coming down here to ballgames when we were kids?" he said. "Eating hot dogs?"

"Trying to catch a foul ball."

When the bed was in place, I grabbed the chains.

"What about it?" I said.

"Nothing. It just seems like a long time ago, longer than it really has been."

"Everything seems like a long time ago." I held up the ends of the chains. "I'm going under."

I got down on the ground and scooted beneath the car. In the half-light of evening, it took me a moment to get the chains hooked onto the undercarriage.

"This is perfect," I said. "It still has the rubber and everything."

I couldn't tell if Vince responded. I thought he said something to acknowledge me, but I couldn't be sure. When I finished, I pushed myself out from under the Saturn and stood up.

Vince stood there, looking past me into the deeper darkness of the alley.

"What?" I said.

He held his finger to his lips.

"Something…"

He took a step past me, a step deeper into the alley.

The tips of my fingers felt cold, and then the chill spread up my arms.

"Go get in the rig," I said.

I pushed the lever. There was a slow grind, and the chain grew taut.

Vince turned.

"I'm on my way," he said. But he stopped almost immediately. "Fuck."

I looked. Someone stood at the end of the rig. In the half-light of the coming evening, the figure was indistinct. It looked to me as though it was leaning against the end of the rig, as if it needed the support to stand up. I couldn't tell if it was a man or a woman. It didn't matter. I pulled the lever, stopping the motion of the Saturn.

"Let's move to the cab," Vince said. "Nice and easy."

"The car's still hooked to the rig."

"I'll get it," he said.

"Let me do it," I said.

"Jett. Get in the cab. I'll be there in a minute."

He didn't leave me a choice. He got down on the

ground.

I started forward, and as I did, the thing—the City Person—at the end of the rig straightened up.

I stopped.

When I was ten, I came face to face with our neighbor's German Shepherd, Schultz. He had bitten other people on our street, and on that particular day, someone had let him out of his fenced-in run. I came around the front of our house, and there was Schultz, standing in our front yard, his nostrils raised to the air as if he smelled fresh meat on the wind.

A distance of seventy-five feet separated me from the front door of our house, and Schultz stood about halfway in between. He had a perfect angle on me if I went for the door.

I didn't know what to do. For some reason, the idea of turning around and going back where I had come from didn't cross my mind. I was too scared, I guess. All I could think about was getting inside the front door, which had always meant coming home and feeling secure.

So I just put my head down and ran. I ran as fast as I could. Schultz didn't even move. He just watched me, silent and still as a post.

Something of that childhood instinct kicked in that day in the alley. I didn't feel as though I had a choice. I ran for the door of the cab, figuring I could move faster than the thing standing by the hood of the rig.

It worked. I reached the cab and pulled the door open before the thing even moved. It took one step toward me, and I pulled the door shut. I had heard that the City People moved slowly, that they walked as if they were half-asleep, and I benefited from that sluggishness.

It was getting darker by this point, and the shadows in the alley made it look almost like full on night. I flipped the headlights on. There were two more of them at the end of the alley, walking our way.

I blasted the horn.

"Vince!"

We kept a crowbar under the front seat for just such an emergency. Vince's idea. I reached under, fumbling through paper cups and fast food wrappers.

"Vince!"

My hand closed around the metal coolness of the crowbar. I slid across the seat and threw the passenger door open.

The City Person that had been out there, the one I had run past like old Schultz, was past the passenger door and moving to the back of the rig toward Vince. He must have heard me coming because he started to turn just as I swung. The crowbar connected with his head with a satisfying thud, and he went down at my feet.

"Vince?"

He rose from beneath the Saturn, his face showing in the darkness.

"Come on, come on!" I said.

I started backward, but Vince didn't move.

Then I saw the hand reaching around his neck.

"No!" I moved forward, raising the crowbar.

"Go," Vince said. His voice sounded hoarse, choking, like he had broken glass in his throat. "Go."

And right there, I did what I always did: I turned and ran. Just like with old Schultz, just like coming back to work. I put my head down and ran for the door of the cab.

And I made it.

The two figures from the end of the alley stood right at the end of the rig. One of them raised its arm.

I thought about reversing, backing the rig up and going for Vince that way.

Then the windshield splintered. They had thrown something at me, and it filled the windshield with an intricate network of spider web cracks, little tributaries that obscured my vision.

I stomped on the accelerator. If the Saturn was still attached, it would be a real short trip for me.

But true to his word, and true to his character, Vince had done his job. I was free of the wreck behind me.

I plowed through the two City People in front of me and out of the alley.

Back to the shed, back to what became the pieces of my life.

The city, in its infinite wisdom, decided not to award a bonus to anyone.

NINE

"You blame yourself for all this," the Kid said.

"You're a master of the obvious," I said. "Who else would I blame?"

"We'll get to that in a minute," he said.

We were still on the side of the road, the rig idling.

"I guess I don't really want to talk about this anymore," I said.

"You didn't do anything unusual," the Kid said. "You did what you had to do to survive."

"Are you okay with that?" I said. "I thought you military guys had a code. Never leave a man behind and all that."

The Kid started laughing. He reached into his pocket and brought out a stick of gum. "You've been watching too many war movies, Chief," he said. "Or you've been watching the news too much. All that duty and honor crap they spoon feed the masses, that's all well and good on a recruiting poster, but in reality...let's just say you're more likely to see the worst of a man on a battlefield than the best of one."

"That doesn't make me feel any better."

"It's not meant to." He rolled down the window and

spit into the street. "How many scandals have come out of the war? Civilians getting shot? Babies getting bombed? Friendly fire?"

Mention of those stories made me squirm. They might have been the reason I stopped watching the news.

"I remember."

"That's your average Joe right there. There aren't any saints or angels."

Marie's phone call came back to me. Her voice was etched in my brain, like a brand. Everywhere I turned, either inside my house or outside, something or someone reminded me of my failure.

"What exactly are you proposing?" I said.

"Go get him. Find him, find his body, and bring it out of there. Let his family have closure. A proper funeral."

"There was a funeral."

"Not a real one. What did you all do, bury an empty casket?"

"There was just a picture. A memorial service."

"That ain't nothing real," the Kid said. "That's just some bullshit. Did it make you feel better?"

"What about the others?" I said. "The other City People out there."

"Collateral damage."

"You said something yesterday about revenge."

"That's right."

"What are you taking revenge on the City People for?" I said.

He reached down and knocked on his leg again.

"That. My ex-girlfriend. The shitty VA hospital. You name it."

"What does that stuff have to do with them?"

"It's connected. Everything's connected."

"Wait," I said. I checked the dashboard clock. We were late, so late. Ned was going to have a fit, but I pushed thoughts of him to the back of my mind. "I'm connected to the City People. They took my friend. You're connected to the war. It took your leg."

"You're not connected to the war?" the Kid said. His eyes widened with disbelief. "You're fueling it. You have your finger on the trigger as much as any of those guys over there. As much as I did. Maybe more."

"More?"

"You could get another job," the Kid said. "If I didn't fight, I'd go to jail. It's all I ever knew. What's your excuse?"

*   *   *

Talking to the Kid always gave me a headache. That day was no exception.

I reached up and rubbed my temple with my left hand. But I'd take the headache over the dreams any day.

"We can do this," I said, "but there have to be some ground rules."

The Kid looked excited. He nearly jumped out of his seat.

"Shoot."

"It can't interfere with work," I said. "The job always comes first. Look how much time we've wasted bullshitting today."

"Fine. Work comes first."

"And I'm the boss. You have to listen to me. None of that wandering off bullshit like yesterday."

"You're the boss. Got it. Is that it?"

There was one more thing. It was the one thing I really didn't like to think about. But I forced myself to say it.

"When the time comes…if the time comes…I want to be the one…with Vince."

73

The Kid nodded.

"You want to deliver the *coup de grace*," he said. "I read you."

It seemed so cold, so brutal to discuss Vince that way. No matter what shape he was in, I didn't want to treat him like a piece of trash.

"Do you think it will come to that?" I said.

"It could, Chief. It very well could. And you," he pointed at me, "have to be willing to finish the job, or we might as well turn around and go home now. Are you up for that, Chief? Can you close the deal?"

"As a last resort, yes."

The Kid nodded his approval. "Good."

"Okay. Now let's get to work." I dropped the rig into gear and we started forward.

"Whatever you say, boss man."

I thought about something else.

"What is it?" the Kid said, as if he could read the look on my face.

"We're going to need a better rig. I don't trust this one."

"Shit, don't sweat that one, chief. Don't sweat that one at all."

*   *   *

We worked it out so that while I hooked up the abandoned car to the rig, the Kid would take a quick look around the block, checking for signs of Vince. It was a good system, since the second man was really along as a lookout and scout anyway. So I did my thing and the Kid did his, and that first day of our quest went by without anything eventful happening. I won't say that I felt comfortable in the city, but the introduction of such a clear purpose — our search for Vince — focused my energies in such a way that my mind didn't dwell so much on the past.

At the end of that day, during our last run, I was hoisting a wreck into place while the Kid wandered across the street and stuck his head into an old drugstore. Its façade was red brick, now stained with soot and crumbling at the edges. Above the store there were windows, and I imagined that at one time the owner lived up there with his family. Safe and secure, without a care in the world.

When the car was up, the Kid stuck his head out the door of the drugstore and called me over.

"Check this out," he said. Then he disappeared back inside.

I followed along behind him, expecting to see more sleeping City People.

When I stepped into the dim light of the store, I saw the Kid standing behind the cash register to the right. Overall, the place wasn't in bad shape. Dusty and dank, but not as trashed as other places I had seen in the city.

The Kid rummaged around behind the counter. In another time, in another life, he might have been the fresh-faced cashier, a young guy working his way through college at a minimum wage job. He must have had the same thought because he popped up with this dopey grin on his face.

"What do you need, sir? Rubbers? Anti-depressants? A porno mag?"

"A partner who does his job," I said. But I was actually getting a kick out of him right then.

"I am doing my job. Recon. The backbone of an army." He raised his hand to his forehead like he was looking over a great distance. "And I got you a present."

"Rubbers?"

"No." He shuffled around in the cash register and

brought out a thick wad of bills, genuine US currency. "What do you think of this?" He dropped them on the counter and fanned them out like a poker hand. I saw a lot of twenties, Andrew Jackson's severe face replicated over and over again. "There must be four, five hundred dollars here."

"Jesus."

"When trouble hit, the owner must have hightailed it. Or else became one of them. Either way, he didn't clean out his drawer. And these City People don't have any use for the money. So…" He ran his hands through the bills on the counter. "We get the booty."

"We're not looters."

"It's not looting. That happened a long time ago. Anything left is fair game. This is just cleaning up the leftovers." He quickly divided the bills into two stacks. "Here."

"No."

"Take it."

"No."

"Jesus. I didn't know you were such a do-gooder, Chief."

"Let's get out of here." But at the door, I stopped. "You know what, I'll take that after all."

The Kid held the two wads of money close to his chest. "You sure? I don't want to corrupt you."

"Give it." I grabbed one of the stacks from his hand.

"Nice," the Kid said. "I like to see that fighting spirit."

"Come on," I said. "Let's get back to work."

TEN

Vince and Marie lived in a three-bedroom ranch about a mile from our house. The neighborhood was full of working people, blue-collar types and some young professionals just starting out. Interest rates were sky high, and nobody was buying or selling houses, except I suppose, the richest of the rich. I didn't know any of them, so I couldn't really speak to that.

Some kids were playing basketball at the end of the street, using a temporary hoop and backboard. Their shouts and huffing breaths reached me as I climbed out of the car.

Gimmetheball, gimmetheball, gimmetheball.

Damn.

Nice shot.

Their house—Marie's house now—had a light burning in the front room, and blue television light flickered off the walls. I hesitated. I knew the house very well. Sometimes it felt as though I had spent as much time there as in our own house. But considering the circumstances of Vince's death and Marie's attitude toward me, I didn't exactly feel welcome.

But since I was there for restitution, I willed myself forward.

In the past, I would have just walked in. I even knew where they kept the spare key — under the ceramic frog in the flower bed — but I couldn't just walk in now.

I knocked, rattling the screen door in its frame.

Andrea, Vince's five-year-old daughter and oldest child, came to the door. She looked tentative. One finger was inserted into her mouth, and she dragged a beat-up looking baby doll behind her. She looked at me like she didn't know me.

"Hi, Andrea," I said through the screen.

"Hi."

She looked just like Vince. Her eyes were big and round with the same intelligence as her dad's. The same eyes I saw pleading with me in my nightmares. It felt like Vince was there, staring back at me.

"It's me. Jett."

She nodded slowly. She knew me, of course. She just wasn't sure what to think of me. Was I the guy who gave her piggyback rides, or was I the monster her mother had been describing to her? How was she to know at age five?

"Is your mom home?"

Andrea didn't respond. She stood in the doorway, studying me, the finger still inserted into her mouth.

"Is she here?" I said.

"Do you know where my daddy is?"

I swallowed hard, but my throat felt like it was stuffed with cotton.

"I…"

"My mommy says you left him somewhere. Do you know where he is?"

"Honey…I…Is your mom home right now?"

She didn't look inclined to move, and I was ready to turn around and forget the whole thing when Marie called from the other room.

"What is it, Andrea?"

In contrast to that hoarse voice from the previous night's phone call, Marie now sounded gentle and soothing, a mother going through her daily life, checking up on her children.

"It's Jett," Andrea said.

"It's what?" Marie appeared in the foyer, the baby in her arms. "Oh."

Her features changed in an instant. Her eyes looked like two pellets of black marble pressed deep into her face.

"I'm sorry to barge in on you like this, but—"

"Andrea. Go in the other room."

"I want to ask Jett something," Andrea said.

"Get in the other room."

Andrea let out a theatrical sigh and walked away, the doll baby bumping against her leg. I really didn't want to hear her question again.

"Marie, I just wanted to bring you something."

She pushed the screen door open. I had to step back and down two steps to avoid getting bashed in the face.

"You've got nerve coming here," she said. "I don't want my children seeing you."

"What have you been telling them about me?" I said. "It's hateful."

"It's the truth. Isn't it?"

"Marie..." The yellow light from the porch cast a sickly glow on us. Their baby, Henry, watched me. He was as peaceful as a Buddha. "I'm grieving too."

"Don't even say that."

"It's true. He didn't belong just to you." I tried to gather my thoughts. "I have dreams about him, Marie. Dreams where he's as real to me as you are right now. He wants something from me in the dream, something he can't say. And in the dream, I'm powerless to do anything to help him. I feel like he's haunting me."

79

"It sounds like real life," she said. "You didn't help him when you left him in the city, either. If you're looking for some kind of absolution, find a priest."

Talking to Marie felt like throwing paper airplanes into a hurricane.

I reached into my pocket. "I brought you this. I know the city benefit program is in the toilet, and they're not paying out as much. I thought you could use it. Take it, it's money."

"I know it's money," she said. "What do you want me to do with it?"

"Buy groceries. Buy toys for the kids."

"And then I'll feel okay? And then I'll mend?"

"I don't know what you'll do," I said.

I was still holding the money out between us. Marie finally reached and took it, and as she gathered it into her hand, some small amount of weight lifted off of me. Even if it was just for a moment, I welcomed that feeling like the end of a long drought.

Marie studied the money in the dim light.

"I know how much you make. You and Nicole can't afford this kind of charity with a new baby."

"Don't worry about that."

Andrea came to the door again.

"Mommy?"

"Go back inside."

"It's Katie. She's crying."

Marie let out a long sigh.

"See my life?" She spoke to Andrea without taking her eyes off me. "Tell her mommy's on the way." Andrea disappeared again. Marie held up the money in the space between us. "This doesn't scratch the surface, you know. Not even close." She stuffed the money into her pocket. "You don't have enough money. No one does."

I should have left right then. I should never have

gone in the first place. A smart man would know when to fold his cards and walk away. But I wasn't smart.

I wanted to make it right.

"I'm going to bring him back," I said.

Marie's brow furrowed.

"What?"

"I'm going to bring Vince back."

"He's gone. No one can bring him back."

"His body," I said. "It's still out there, and I'm going to bring it back. I'm going to end this, for all of us."

Her features softened just a bit, and I thought for a moment that something had gotten through to her, that all of a sudden we understood each other in a way I had previously only hoped for.

But then the stack of bills smacked me in the face, thrown with all the force Marie could muster while her other arm held the baby. While the money fluttered to the ground, Marie pulled the door open and went inside, but she took the time to walk back and yell at me through the screen.

"Do you think this can end?" she said. "Do you think this can ever, *ever* end?"

Her voice cut through the night like an alarm. I thought about gathering up the money on her porch, but decided to leave it. She might change her mind in the morning.

The basketball players had stopped their game. I knew they had heard Marie's excoriation of me.

They watched me in the dark, their eyes on my back as heavy and powerful as the world's judgment.

*   *   *

At home, I found our house satisfyingly quiet. From time to time, depending on how long a day it had been,

Nicole fell asleep right after putting Sophie down for the night. Since I was ninety minutes late, I hoped that was the case.

I walked from the garage into the kitchen, which was clean and devoid of any sign that a meal had recently been eaten there. I wasn't hungry anyway. The overhead light was off, and the lone bulb under the microwave provided a soft glow that suggested the day's work was done. I opened the refrigerator and found a can of beer. I opened it at the kitchen table and sipped it in the half-light.

I had taken a few drinks and felt the first tinglings of a buzz at the base of my skull.

"You're late."

I jumped a little. I didn't see Nicole come to the doorway. "You scared me," I said. "Jesus."

She wore sweatpants and a baggy T-shirt. She didn't look like she'd been sleeping. "I heard you come in," she said.

"Is Sophie asleep?"

"Half an hour ago." She came over to the table and pulled a chair out on the other side. We had bought the table before we were married. A lot of words had gone back and forth over its top, a lot of meals eaten. "Everything okay at work today?" she said.

"Sure. We ran a little late. But we were safe. Don't worry."

She smiled, but it looked forced, like someone was pulling the corners of her mouth up with invisible wires. "I do worry, though."

"I know. I worry about the two of you. I really do. Have you been keeping the doors locked?"

"Yes. Of course."

"I was thinking we should move Sophie's crib back into our room. That way she could be a lot closer to us if there was trouble. We would hear her better."

I reached for her hand across the tabletop, but she pulled back.

"Are you sure nothing else happened at work today?" she said. "Nothing you need to tell me about?"

"It's fine," I said. "Nic, we didn't take any risks."

The smile, such as it was, faded from her face. "Marie called just before you came in. In fact, I was on the phone with her when I heard you downstairs."

Nothing ever made me feel more like a child than being caught in a lie. My shoulders slumped.

"She was telling me that you brought her money," Nicole said. "A big wad of cash. Blood money, she called it."

"Nicole."

"No." She held up her finger. "No, just listen." She shook her head, a gesture that resembled a shudder. "You gave her our money, Jett. We don't have money to give away to people. Sophie needs clothes, she's due at the doctor—"

"It wasn't our money."

"Whose money was it?"

"I'd rather not tell you."

"That's good, Jett. Real good." She looked away from me, her eyes misting. "I don't know which is worse, lying or secrets. At least with a lie, I can convince myself you're trying to protect me or something. But the secrets...the things you do at work, the things you see in your sleep. To think there are things in your life you don't want to tell me. I don't understand that."

"Nicole..."

"She told me something else." She wiped at the corner of her left eye with her index finger. "She said you told her you were going after Vince, that you were going to get his body back for her and take it away from those

City People. Why would you say something like that to her?"

"Because I'm going to do it."

"No. You can't do that. Why would you?"

"Because it's my fault he's out there."

"No, no." Nicole leaned forward. Her hands were warm, and she covered mine with hers. Her voice softened. "No, Jett. What happened out there was an accident. That's all it was, an accident. You can't do this to yourself. You've been tying yourself up in knots since Vince died. You're driving yourself crazy with this stuff."

She stood up and came around to my side of the table. She draped her arms around my back and shoulders. I felt her hair tickle against the skin of my neck.

"It's not your fault," she said.

It was the most intimate, meaningful contact we had shared in weeks. I felt something give inside me, and I wanted very badly to wish that the world was the way she saw it. I reached up and squeezed her hand.

Then the phone rang, and we jumped.

"Jesus," I said.

"I'll get it," Nicole said. She released her grip on my hand. "If it's Marie, I'm telling her to go fuck herself."

She went across the room and answered. She told the person to hold on just a minute then extended the receiver toward me. "It's work," she said.

"Ned?"

"I don't know who it is."

I took the phone. "Hello?"

"Hey, Chief, sorry to interrupt your domestic bliss."

"What are you calling for?"

"Easy, Chief. I'm about to change your life."

Nicole looked at me, curiosity on her face. I hoped she would wander out of the room and check on Sophie, but she sat at the table and waited for me to finish.

84

"Was that your wife who answered the phone?"

"Yeah."

"She sounds like a keeper, Chief. Nice voice. Good phone manners."

"Cut to the chase, what do you want?"

"Sure, sure. You have a date with the wife? Making another little Chief over there?" He laughed into the phone, and I had to move it away from my ear. "Listen, I was just calling to say I have a surprise for you. Something that'll make you happy and make our job a lot easier."

"I'm listening."

"No, you'll find out tomorrow. And you can thank me then. Just remember, the Kid is looking out for you."

I was about to tell him I didn't like surprises, that I had had enough of them recently to turn me off to them forever, but he'd already hung up. I held the receiver to my ear until the dial tone clicked on.

"What was that about?" Nicole asked.

I hung up the phone. "Just work stuff."

"Who was it?"

I couldn't lie. "That guy I told you about, my new partner."

"What did he want?"

I came to the table and sat down. "You don't under-stand something. That was my original new partner, the one I first told you about."

"The guy from the war?"

"Right."

"I thought you asked for a new partner."

"I did. But then I asked for this guy back."

"You said he was an idiot."

"He is. But he's...helpful in a certain way."

Nicole studied me from across the table. She was working through something. "Is he the one getting you involved in all this? This stuff with Vince? And the money?"

"He's not getting me involved in anything. I want to do these things. I need to."

She stood up and pushed her chair back under the table. "You know how I said earlier that I didn't know which was worse, the lies or the secrets? I know the answer to that question now."

"And that is?"

"I like the lies better. And do you know why? Because the truth scares the hell out of me."

ELEVEN

Ned intercepted me on my way to the break room the next morning. He wore a puzzled, almost bemused expression on his face.

"I just got the strangest phone call," he said. No hello, no greeting. "I'm not sure what to make of it."

"What happened?"

"It's McGruder. He's not coming to work today. He's in the hospital."

"Jesus. What for?"

Ned scratched his head.

"Apparently, somebody jumped him outside of his apartment last night. They got him as he walked in from his car. He's busted all to hell. Broken collarbone, concussion, smashed teeth. Shit, I don't even remember what all they said was wrong with him. But he's not coming to work. Not today, not for a long time."

Crime had gone up as the city fell apart. It wasn't unusual for people to be mugged, their wallets taken. Even a few bucks could entice someone desperate. But usually it wasn't as violent as Ned made this attack sound.

"Did they catch the guy?"

"I don't know. I doubt it. They never catch people for those things." He shook his head. "We really need to step it up with him gone."

"We can do it," I said, although the words sounded false as I spoke them. My can-do spirit was as stale as last month's bread. I only cared about my own problems: my marriage, my guilt.

"We'll have to," Ned said. "And you're going to lead the way. Why don't you take McGruder's rig back. It would have been yours anyway if not for...all that trouble."

"What about the other guys?" I said. "Guys like Bobby Crawford. Shouldn't they move up?"

"You take it." He gave me an awkward clap on the shoulder. "You're back on top, Jett. Go get 'em."

* * *

The Kid stood by the number one rig, his good foot propped on the running board on the passenger side. His grin looked like a shark's.

As I walked up, I thought back to his phone call from the night before, and his promise of a surprise. Some things began to coalesce in my brain.

"How did you know we had this truck?" I said.

"A little bird told me. Actually, the little bird said, 'Stop hitting me. Jesus. You're going to kill me. Take my wallet and keys. Take everything.' But I knew what it meant." He pointed to the rig. "Surprise."

I didn't have enough desire to give voice to my outrage. "I knew it," was all I could manage. Still, the better rig meant a better chance of finding Vince. I had cast my lot with the Kid, so I just walked around to the driver's side and climbed in. "Let's go."

*   *   *

"Why so glum, Chief?" the Kid said.

We were searching the area near the old Music Hall, a venue that used to host operas and symphonies, but was now a crumbling brick shell, its box office windows smashed, the rustic, cobblestone street out front overgrown with weeds.

"I'm tired."

"Ah. You did have a date with the wife last night."

"Hardly. I slept on the couch. My neck's killing me."

"Sleeping on the couch. Let me guess, your wife doesn't like me very much. She thinks I'm a bad influence on you."

"Do you do marriage counseling on the side? I mean in addition to smashing the skulls of work rivals."

"I just know that people don't like me. I was always the one who other parents would tell their kids to stay away from. I can't tell you how many yards I was banned from growing up. I have that effect on people."

"It's a gift like anything else," I said.

"It works for you. You like having me around."

"I'm using you for a very specific purpose."

"Shit, I'm a soldier. I've been used and abused by bigger dogs than you."

*   *   *

And for the next several weeks, the Kid and I used each other.

I fed off of his courage, his aura of invincibility. Perhaps it was his experience in combat, or maybe it was something deeper and more essential to his character, but the Kid never showed fear or doubt, never acted as though any step he took could lead him into mortal danger. I followed him every step of the way, drafting in his wake, convincing myself that his confidence and certainty also enfolded and protected me. As long as I was with him, and stepping in his tracks, no harm would fall on me, and we would bring Vince home together.

Our days together went like this: we spent the mornings doing our regular work, scouting for cars and bringing them back to the shed for crushing. We worked together well, and as a team, we almost worked up to the lofty standards set by Vince and me. I had expected trouble from the Kid, but he went along with the regular work all morning, rarely wandering off. And if he did wander, I brought him back just by calling.

His pliancy made me uneasy. I suspected all along that he was building to something, but maybe the way we spent our afternoons released whatever pressure built within him. During the afternoons, we gave ourselves over to the Kid's way of doing business, and his agenda of revenge on the nameless and faceless demons of the world became my agenda as well.

TWELVE

Ostensibly, we were looking for Vince.

We ate lunch with the other drivers, just like the regular guys we pretended to be, then we headed back out in our rig and scoured the abandoned buildings and empty storefronts looking for my lost partner.

But we didn't find him. No sign or trace of him.

But we did find a lot of City People, snoozing away the long afternoons in their stuporous haze. When we found them, we destroyed them.

At first, I let the Kid do most of the bashing. He liked it, of course, and killing, or whatever we were doing to those beings, came to him easily. He could destroy one of their heads one minute then talk to me about the weather or the chances that we were ever going to get a cost-of-living raise in the next. It didn't appear to shake him or give him pause. He beat in the head of a City Person and turned it to mush with the same nonchalance I would feel about stepping on a bug.

I couldn't do it like he could.

I couldn't stop thinking about that first day, that City Person whose head I crushed in the liquor store. I had never experienced a lack of control like that, and I wasn't eager to experience it again. On that day, it was as though I walked up to an abyss, and while I didn't completely lose my balance and go over the side, I came close. Perilously close. And my fear was that if I approached the abyss again, I would be powerless to stop myself from going all the way over. And there didn't appear to be any coming back once that happened.

I thought that about the Kid. Something about the war, something about his injuries, had sent him to a place he couldn't come back from. I wasn't keen to join him.

But with the Kid, there were never really choices. With him, it was all or nothing. That gave him his strength, I think, and it also made him dangerous.

*   *   *

One week into our odyssey, we stopped at an abandoned house. It was two stories, brick, the windows, of course, smashed to pieces, the empty frames staring back at us like gouged out eyes.

We stepped inside. The sun was bright that afternoon, and enough light came through the windows to render the flashlight beam unnecessary. The living room/dining room that stretched across the front of the house was empty, except for scattered old magazines and beer bottles, the detritus of a life that wasn't being lived anymore.

We moved down a short hallway to the kitchen, and there the flashlight became a necessity. The kitchen window faced another building across an alley, and less light fell through there. I flicked the beam on, and we saw the woman lying under the kitchen table. She must have been about fifty, and while her transformation into a City Person hadn't done her any favors, it was obvious that even before that she had lived a difficult life. Her face was deeply lined, her stringy hair thinning. She was scrawny and sickly, like a junkie or a drunk or both.

"She's not going anywhere," the Kid said. "Let's check upstairs."

We did and found nothing. The bedrooms were empty, the faucet in the bathroom still stubbornly dripping water long after anyone had any inclination to use it. I hated the thought of the waste, so I tightened it. The stream didn't stop, but it slowed some. We went back downstairs.

I started for the door, leaving the Kid to his work in the kitchen. His voice stopped me. "Hold it, Chief."

"What?"

He waved me back, but I didn't move.

"What?" I said again.

"I need your help in the kitchen."

"Do you need the light?" I said, holding the flashlight toward him.

"Come on," he said.

I followed him down the hall to the kitchen, retracing the steps we had taken earlier. The flashlight beam filled the room, illuminating the woman in her place underneath the table. I held the beam on her.

"Okay," I said.

The Kid bent down and grabbed a fistful of the woman's raggedy dress. He pulled her from underneath the table until she was in the middle of the floor. The woman groaned, a low, sleepy sound, but otherwise lay still as a post on the dirty linoleum.

"Here." The Kid held the tire iron out to me.

"What are you doing?" I said.

He smiled.

"I'm not doing anything, Chief. You are." He pointed at the woman. "Terminate her. With extreme prejudice."

A wave of hostility came off the Kid, something that

simmered beneath his words, like a hot gust of wind on a summer day.

"I thought you wanted to kill them," I said.

"I do. And I will. But not this one." He still held the tire iron out between us. "I thought of something. This is a pretty sweet deal for you, isn't it? I do all the dirty work. If we ever get caught, you can play dumb, say that I was the one doing the killing and you didn't have anything to do with it."

"I wouldn't do that."

"Bullshit, Chief. You can say you wouldn't, but you don't know. You already left one partner behind. How do I know you won't do that to me?"

"You're going to throw that back at me."

"Look. It's nothing personal. It's business. Let's just say I've been in these arrangements before, and somebody always lacks the balls to finish the job. And somebody else, usually the lower ranking guy, ends up being the sacrificial lamb." He jiggled the tire iron. "This is insurance. For me."

I reached out and took the tire iron. I traded the flashlight for it.

The Kid pointed the beam down at the woman. I took a hesitant step forward.

"I know you can do it, Chief. You did it that one day."

I stopped.

"I was angry that day. Something flowed through me, and I couldn't stop myself."

The Kid nodded.

"That feeling is your friend," he said. "Now just step over there and think about all the shit going wrong in your life. Your lost partner, the fight with your old lady, your bills, your fears for your daughter. Roll them all up and put them right on her head."

My first swing didn't do anything. It barely marked

her.

The woman grunted and squirmed, but made no move to defend herself.

"Harder," the Kid said.

I swung again, putting more force behind it. The thump was louder, deeper. Her skin split along the forehead. I brought the tire iron down again and again, and with each successive blow, the Kid urged me on. And with each blow, it got easier to do. The anger flowed through me more naturally, so much so that I didn't notice the spraying fluids and chunks of skin and brain that hit me in the face. I must have swung the iron ten times until there was next to nothing left of the woman's head, until it would have been generous to call what was left of her human remains.

I stopped myself this time when I ran out of breath.

I looked over at the Kid who was nodding and grinning.

"Welcome to the war, Chief," he said. "Next time, don't stand so close, and then you won't go home wearing her brains as an accessory."

THIRTEEN

On one of those afternoons, Ned stopped me after I clocked out.

He asked if I had time to talk to him in his office. I carried another wad of cash in my pocket, money that the Kid liberated from a grocery store down on 11th Street, and I was eager to take it to Marie and then get home before I caused more disruptions with Nicole.

But Ned almost looked like he wanted to cry, so I agreed to talk to him.

I followed him to his office and sat down.

He had an extra large soda cup from a fast food restaurant on his desk. He brought it up to his mouth and took a long pull through the straw.

"What's up?" I said.

Ned let out a small burp. "I'm a little concerned about your productivity," he said. "Your numbers have been slipping for the last two weeks."

It wasn't a complete surprise to hear Ned say this. I expected he would start complaining at some point.

"We're in a little dry patch," I said. "It'll be fine."

"Is it the partner?" he said. "I know you took him on as a special project, but he doesn't have to stay."

"No," I said. "It's not him. We'll bounce back. Don't worry."

My ability to tell people things they wanted to hear had reached new heights.

"I hope so." He stifled another burp. "Because I'm getting some heat from above on this. The numbers are down, but demand is up. With McGruder down..."

"How is he?"

"He's going to be out for awhile. He may not ever be able to come back here to work. He might have to go to a desk job." Ned shrugged. "I'm afraid that if we don't pick it up, they're going to tell me to let some guys go. They'll bring in people from other departments to drive. Your partner might be one of the first ones to go. Last hired, first fired."

"You won't have to do that," I said. "We'll pick it up."

"I hope so."

I felt the unnatural bulk of the wad of cash in my pocket. The Kid had more to do for me. And for Vince and Marie. He couldn't be fired.

"It's done," I said. "Don't worry about it."

*   *   *

When I rang the bell at Marie's house that night, no one answered. There were lights on in the back of the house, but no one came to the door.

I didn't blame them if they didn't want to see me, but I didn't know if the money would be safe if I just left it in the mailbox.

I rang the bell a last time, and was turning around, when I heard the locks being undone from the inside. I waited. They must have had five different chains and locks to undo, and I didn't blame them for that, being a single mother and her kids in this world.

When the door opened, it was Marie who looked out at me.

"Oh," she said. "It's you."

I brought out the wad of cash.

"We don't have to talk. I just wanted you to have this. There's a few hundred bucks there."

She stared at the wad of cash for a brief moment then took it. She didn't look at it or count it.

"Good night," I said.

"Do you know what we're doing in here?" she said.

I stopped, halfway down the steps and shook my head.

"We're watching home videos, me and the kids. Birthday parties. Christmas. Stuff like that."

Her voice lacked the edge it had on my previous visit. It almost seemed as though she wanted to talk to me.

"That sounds nice," I said.

"You're all over them," she said. "You. Nicole. Sophie. You're everywhere. It's like your part of the fabric of who we are."

"I guess that's true. We feel the same way about all of you."

Marie nodded. She looked down at the money and slid it into her pants pocket.

The night was a little cool. When the breeze picked up, Marie pulled her sweater tighter around her body and let the sleeves fall over her hands.

"I better be going," I said.

"I knew it was going to be you at the door, Jett. As soon as it rang, I knew you'd be here with some more of that money. God only knows where you get it from." She sniffled. "And do you know what I thought when I first saw your face?"

"What?"

"I thought that I should just invite you in here with

us. We could watch those stupid videos together, watch Vince and you and everybody else, the way we used to be. Hell, we could even cry together if we wanted."

She was holding something back, so I tried to prompt her.

"That sounds nice, Marie. We could do that sometime."

She shook her head. "No, we couldn't. That's just it. We couldn't. We couldn't act like we were friends, and everything was back to normal."

"Why not?"

"Because every time I'd look at you or Sophie or Nicole, I'd know what I've lost, and what you still have. I couldn't do that. It's easier for me to look at these videos and see Vince than it is for me to see you."

"I'm sorry, Marie."

"Not half as sorry as I am," she said.

I didn't agree with that statement, but I wasn't going to argue either.

Marie let the screen door go, but stopped it before it closed all the way. "If you bring any more of this money by, Jett, just leave it in the mailbox. I won't be opening the door to you anymore."

FOURTEEN

."We're just going to have to slow down for awhile," I said.

We were out on patrol, in the morning, and we had already grabbed two nice vehicles and brought them back to the shed. The Kid jabbered away about how sweet it was to be back in business, to be on maneuvers again.

"You know what, Chief?" he said. "You would have made a damn fine soldier yourself. Really. No shit. You take orders well, and you're not afraid to get down and dirty with it when the situation dictates."

"Kid? Are you listening to me at all?"

"I can hear you," he said. "I don't know that I'm exactly listening."

"My daughter has more sense than you."

We turned north on Poplar Street for a block and then made a turn east. We didn't have a real direction in mind. We were freelancing, scouting for more scrap. The sky was overcast, the color of iron. The winds had picked up, scattering papers and trash in our path.

Mention of Sophie turned my thoughts back to the home front. I wondered if they wouldn't be better off without me and the burdens I carried around. I thought about times in the past, times before everything changed. I had thought we were safe in our little lives, protected from the tides that knocked and buffeted the rest of the world. I was so naïve and so wrong.

"You know what?" the Kid said. "Fuck Ned. He's a pantywaist. He's like a little girl, always crying and worrying about getting in trouble."

"If he fires you, we won't be able to do any of this. Our whole deal is off. You need city credentials to get into the city and do any of this."

"I don't need city credentials." The Kid sounded pouty. "There are other ways. I've been looking into some of them."

"Oh really?"

"Yeah. You think there's only one way to do something, Mr. Straight-and-Narrow? There are always alternatives."

I felt like I was talking to a brick wall.

"Can you just do it for me?" I said. "For a few days, can we concentrate on work and get Ned off our backs? I don't want to lose my job."

"Stop!"

"What?"

"Stop," the Kid said again. "Damn it."

I hit the brakes. "What do you see?"

"There," he said. "Right there."

"A City Person?"

"No," he said. "In the alley. A car, a nice one."

A sky blue Mercury, in nearly pristine condition, sat in the mouth of the alley.

"Nice see," I said.

"You wanted work put first. Remember?" The Kid reached under his seat for the tire iron. "And you think I don't listen to you."

But I had already tuned the Kid out. The scene, of course, reminded me of Vince's death. A nice-looking car in the alley. It would also require us to back in, to go into the alley to hook everything up. And the car looked unlike most of the wrecks we encountered. It seemed almost too good to be true.

"Are you going to back in?"

I raised a finger to silence him.

"Hold it. Something's not right."

"What?"

"I'm not sure. Will you grab the bat, too?"

"Rock on," the Kid said.

I stepped down into the street. The wind whipped the pants legs of my coveralls around. The Kid came to my side of the rig with the bat in one hand and the tire iron in the other.

"You see enemy movement?" he said.

"I don't know. What do you think of all of this?"

"It's a sweet pick up. It would help keep that cow Ned off our backs for another day."

"This is exactly how Vince went down. A car in an alley. It looks the same."

"You having some sort of flashback, Chief?"

"I think you could call it that."

It was more than a flashback. It was the scene of my nightmares come to life.

The Kid held the bat out to me. "Let's get in there. Back that rig in, and we'll do our business."

I stopped him by placing my hand on his arm. "I think we should get out of here." I stepped back toward the rig. The Kid didn't move. He stood there in the street with the tire iron in his hand. He knocked it against his palm, like a beat cop with his nightstick.

"No," he said. "Come on. Let's look."

"Kid…"

He came over toward me. "When I was in the war, we had to check this stuff out. You can't just walk away from a chance to know your enemy better." He looked toward the alley, then back at me. "I have a feeling this will pay off."

"What if it's a trap?" I said.

"Then we know going in," he said. "We have the advantage now."

In contrast to the Kid's good feeling, I had a bad one. A tightening in my chest. A tingling in my palms. But he didn't give me a chance to object, and I was slow to find my voice.

"Pull the rig around," he said. "Just like normal."

While I did that, backing and lining up with the car in the alley, the Kid stood in the street peering past the parked car, trying to see if there was any movement or sign of trouble. When I climbed down from the cab, his face looked worried, the deep lines around his frown of concentration the only sign of age he had ever shown.

"What's the story?"

"All quiet on the western front," he said.

I stood on my tiptoes and looked down the alley. Nothing but darkness and quiet. The car wasn't as far down the alley as the day Vince died. "Maybe we're being paranoid," I said.

The Kid looked at me like I was simple. "Chief, the only good way to be these days is paranoid." He pointed to the car and the rig. "You want to do your thing while I stand guard?"

I lowered the bed and grabbed the chains while the Kid stood at parade rest, the tire iron ready to bash anything that might cause us harm. In many ways, I didn't trust the Kid, but for some reason, I did believe he would protect me. Not that he cared in any significant way for me or my well-being. It wasn't that. It was just that something about his presence made me feel safer, like having a large, muscular friend by your side in a bar brawl.

"Do you really think it could be a trap?" he asked.

"I don't know. It seems far-fetched. After all, their brains are destroyed. How could they think something like that through?"

"I have some thoughts on that subject."

"What thoughts?"

"Later," he said. "When we're in the clear."

I got down on the ground and hooked the chains to the undercarriage, then pulled the lever. The car slowly moved into place. When it was loaded, I looked at the Kid. "You ready?"

He was still looking down the alley. He looked disappointed that something hadn't happened, that he didn't get the engagement he desired. "Yeah, I guess so."

"Then let's go. I don't like standing around here. I've had enough of this."

But the Kid didn't move. His eyes were narrowed, and I could almost hear the gears turning around in his head, a slow grinding like the insides of a clock.

He took a couple of steps toward the back of the rig and looked up at the car on the bed. "You read a lot in high school, Chief?"

"What?"

"Did you read a lot in high school? You know, Shakespeare, Milton, all of that bullshit?"

"I read some of it. Why, you want to start a book club?"

He kept his eyes on the car. "Did you ever read Homer? You know, the *Iliad*, the one about the Trojan War?"

"I think I read the Cliff's Notes."

"It's a good one," he said. "All about war and honor

and soldiers. I couldn't get enough of it." He took a couple of steps back from the rig. "Lower this thing to the ground again, will you?"

"Why?"

"Just do it. Something ain't right, and I think I know what it is."

I did as he asked, pushed the lever and lowered the bed back to the ground, putting the car at a forty-five degree angle to the street.

"Stop there," he said. He stood in the alley, looking up at the car.

"What's going on, Kid?"

"You know what a Trojan Horse is, don't you, Chief?"

And then I understood what he was driving at.

"Let's dump it and go," I said, my voice a hoarse whisper.

"No," the Kid said. He pointed up at the car. "We've got them right where we want them."

He was right. The angle of the car meant that anyone inside would have a difficult time getting out without falling. We had the advantage.

"What are you going to do?"

The Kid ran his tongue over his lips. "Grab your bat."

I had leaned the bat against the side of the rig. I picked it up, my palm slick against the handle. "What's the plan?"

"Come here."

I moved to his side.

"I'm just going to reach up here and yank this door open," he said. "If anyone is in there, we'll see them and finish them."

He reached up, stretching his body out to its full length, but his hand came just short of the driver's side door handle. "You're going to have to do it," he said. "You're taller than me. Reach up there and open that door."

I moved closer to the rig. I stretched out as far as I could go, extending my left hand, which shook as it took hold of the door handle. I tugged and pulled and the door swung open, then bounced right back and closed again.

"Did you see anything?" I said.

"Too fast. Do it again and stick the bat in there to prop it open."

"Let's just cut it loose and get out of here."

"Bullshit. Do it."

"When did I start taking orders from you?"

"You handle the work side, I handle the war side," he said. He tightened the grip on the tire iron and raised it back and above his head. "Now do it."

I reached up again. This time, when I grabbed the handle and threw the door open, I brought the bat around, just like the Kid said, and caught the door before it slammed shut. I had to wrestle with it a little bit, but I managed to keep it open wide enough for the Kid to look inside the front seat. He even jumped up in the air to get a better look.

"All clear," he said. "Now do the back."

I repeated the move on the back door. It was easier because the rear of the car was closer to the ground. And I had already done it once.

We had the same result. The Kid looked and declared it all clear. "Okay," he said. "Let's check the trunk."

He tilted his head, indicating that I should follow him to the back of the rig. I did. When we moved back there, I looked at him. "How are you going to get that open?"

He shrugged. "No problem. I know how to break into things."

"Why does this not surprise me?"

He took the flat end of the tire iron, the one not

designed to tighten or loosen lug nuts, and wedged it into the space where the trunk met the rest of the car. He worked it in a little bit, his upper teeth biting down on his lower lip, then nodded at me.

"You've got my back, Chief. When this thing goes up, be ready to swing."

I nodded.

"Ready?"

"Ready."

With a small grunt, the Kid levered the tire iron and popped the trunk lid up.

The lid and the buildings on either side of us cast a shadow over the trunk, and for a moment, I couldn't make anything out. Then something made a scuffling sound. There was movement. I saw the outline of a body. Two bodies.

I swung the bat at the head, but the City Person was wedged against the side of the trunk, its head protected by the metal frame of the car. My bat made contact with the car, a metallic crunch, but it didn't touch the City Person. I swung again and again but couldn't get the angle right to make contact with the head. I was just bashing the car.

"Back off," the Kid said. He sounded disgusted.

He moved in, tire iron raised, and started swinging in swift arcs against the City Person's body, the iron making a whistling sound against the air as he brought it down again and again. When he paused, I told him I was going to cut the car loose so we could go.

"Bullshit. We're here to finish."

He reached into the trunk and grabbed a fistful of clothing. He pulled, lifting the City Person partway out of the trunk. "Help me, damn it."

I grabbed a hold, too, and we managed to drag the body out of the trunk and drop it in the street.

It was a man, about the same age as the Kid, and he rolled over on his face as if the sight of the day and our faces blinded him.

It took the Kid mere seconds to finish him off. Three precise blows to the head, and it was done. The Kid wasn't even breathing heavy. "Let's get the other one," he said.

We reached in and took hold of it.

"Careful you don't get bit," I said.

"Fuck that."

We pulled. This one was lighter, and only when we had it out on the street and lying at our feet did we see why. The woman was about twenty years old, wearing a skirt and sandals. Her hair, dirty and matted, was long enough to reach halfway down her back.

The Kid reached down and took a fistful of that hair. "Look at this bitch," he said. "Just waiting to take us down."

The woman grimaced under the Kid's touch, the most reaction I had ever seen from one of them. She kicked her legs to get away. Without the Kid asking, I bent down and pinned them with my hands, forcing her to lie still in the alley.

"Do it," I said. "Get it over with."

But the Kid wasn't listening. He leaned in close to the squirming woman and spoke close to her ear. "Look at this bitch," he said. "Mister and Missus City Motherfucker waiting to take us down."

"Don't fuck around," I said.

"You ever wonder what it might be like to fuck one of these bitches?" he said. "You think she can still get wet? You think she can still suck somebody off?"

"Jesus." I let go of her feet and grabbed the bat. Being careful not to hit the Kid, I brought the bat down against her head.

"Goddamnit, Jett!"

But I kept on swinging until her head was unrecognizable.

I looked up. The Kid was glaring at me. "What the fuck did you do that for?"

"We've got to get out of here. We've got to get back and warn the others."

I let the car back down and unhooked the chains. The Kid just stood there, looking down at the two City People. He only moved when he had to, when the car backed over them with a series of dull thumps.

"Come on," I said.

He still didn't move.

"Kid. *Come on.*"

He looked up at me, his eyes full of hate. "I'm coming," he said. "But I'm not doing that again."

"Doing what? Touching them?"

The Kid looked down at the bodies again, then back up at me. "No," he said. "I'm not going to let you stop me so easily."

FIFTEEN

I didn't have time to digest everything the Kid had said and done in the alley. I was more concerned with practical matters, like getting our asses out of harm's way. And getting back to base and warning the others.

As we drove, the Kid seemed to calm down. The wild look in his eye dimmed, and the flush left his cheeks.

"How did you know they were in there?" I said.

He didn't answer right away. He looked lost in his own thoughts.

"Kid?"

"Just a feeling, I guess. From combat. Over there, it got so we knew when an attack was coming. I could sense something, like an electrical charge. The air sort of crackles right before something happens."

"And you still went right into it? And brought me along?"

"You don't always have a choice," he said. "We could know an attack was coming and still have to go into it. You're not going to find your partner by sitting on the sidelines. And we got them. Did you see that? We took two of them down."

We passed through the checkpoint, allowing us out of

the city. I considered reporting what we saw to the military guys, but something in the Kid's mood told me we had more to talk about before we shared our story with anybody else.

"What the hell was going on back there?" I said.

"I don't know," the Kid said. "They were trying to get out. Sit in the trunk, we take them out, and then at night, they could use the trunk release to get away. Presto. They're out of the city."

"What if the car goes right into the crusher?"

"Chief, we've already determined that foot soldiers are expendable. You think they expected every guy who landed on Normandy or Iwo Jima to walk away unscathed?"

"You think they've done this before?"

"I don't think they woke up this morning and got a wild hair," he said. "You might have been shuttling them out for weeks and didn't even know it."

His words gave me a sick feeling in my stomach.

We came in sight of the shed. I guided the rig into the lot and parked in our familiar spot, but it didn't feel as safe or familiar as it once had. Something fundamental had shifted.

We didn't get out of the cab. We sat there while the engine ticked and cooled. Our co-workers came and went, oblivious.

"We have to tell them," I said. "We have to tell everybody."

"Just hold your water a minute," the Kid said. We remained in the cab of the rig. "Let's not fly off the handle."

"If it's a trap, these guys are in danger."

"What if it isn't? What if it's random?"

"Do you believe that?" I said.

"No, I don't. And other people don't either."

"What other people? People who work here?"

"No. But I've been talking to people and doing some research. I've learned a few things."

"What happened to no secrets between partners?"

"I'm protecting you," he said. "People already think you're a little loopy. What if you start talking about this stuff without any proof to back it up? They'll really think you're around the bend and off the mountain." He put his hand on the door handle. "Just keep quiet until after lunch. I'm going to check on something."

"Where are you going?" I asked.

"Trust me," he said. "I have an idea."

"Trust *you*? Did you really just say that?"

"I did, Chief."

I looked out at the gray sky. A lone bird, high and wheeling, rose and fell, buffeted by the winds. "You know that tingling feeling you get before an attack?"

"Sure."

"I get it whenever you say 'Trust me.'"

*　　*　　*

The Kid and I normally ate lunch in the break room. Over ham sandwiches and potato chips, we would talk with the other drivers who happened to be around. The Kid laughed a lot and told a lot of stories about the war, most of them humorous, some of them bloody. The content didn't matter. The other guys always had the same reaction to the Kid. They laughed at his stories if they were funny, or shook their heads if the story was sad, but when the Kid wasn't looking, they all had the same look in their eyes. It was a look that said they feared him, that here was a walking, talking hand grenade, and the pin had long ago been pulled and discarded.

They gave me looks, too, when they made eye contact

with me. Initially they gave me pity because of Vince. Now they looked at me with incomprehension because I had asked to be put back on with the Kid. Whatever malady they suspected of him had now been transferred to me, and I too was an object of suspicion and unease.

That day, after our run-in with the Trojan Horse, I sat at a table with Bobby Crawford, Travis Coffey, and Mike Clark. They had worked there as long as me, some of them longer. They nodded to me when I sat down, mumbled hellos around mouthfuls of their food. I was shaken, my insides like cold jelly.

"Where's that partner of yours, Jett?" Bobby asked.

I heard a trace of derision in his voice.

"On an errand," I said. "He'll be back."

"How's he working out?" Coffey asked. "He seems a little squirrelly."

Somebody at the table made a snorting noise, something akin to laughter. I didn't see who it was.

"He's okay. He pulls his weight. He was in the war, you know. Lost half his leg."

They all nodded. I thought I had scored points with them there. Who could criticize a guy who gave half his leg in the war? None of us had served.

I kept on chewing, hoping we were finished talking about the Kid. I wanted to bring up a topic, but there wasn't much to talk about these days. At one time, I remembered talking about sports at work, but the professional leagues had gone on hiatus in the wake of the war. Politics was out of the question since all politicians were crooks or worse. The weather hadn't turned yet. And I didn't want to talk about me and my problems at home.

Coffey cleared his throat.

"I appreciate him being in the war and all that," he said. "I got a brother over there, as I'm sure you remember."

I nodded. "I do."

Coffey nodded back. He was a good worker. Not the best but very good, and I liked him. He took a long drink from a bottle of Pepsi. "It's just that some of those boys don't come back from over there quite right in the head." He pointed to his own temple. "You know what I mean?"

"You're saying the Kid's crazy?"

He cleared his throat again. "I've got a buddy who works over in human resources at city hall. He told me that some of these guys the city's been hiring ain't exactly of the soundest mind."

"How do you mean?"

"He didn't name any names. He didn't know the names. But he said some of these guys have been involved in some shit over there that most of us would prefer not to know about. And rather than face the music from the army, and expose a big scandal, they just dismissed these boys and sent them back to the States where they were given nice jobs where they couldn't hurt anybody."

"You're full of it."

"He didn't say it was the Kid," Bobby said. "He said it *could* be the Kid. Could be."

"My buddy knows for certain that one of those guys was sent to work here." Coffey shrugged. "We got three new guys that way. Who do you think it is?"

"But you didn't have the name?"

"My buddy told me he could find out, if we really wanted him to. He'd have to dig around, ask the right people. But he thinks he could tell us, if you want to know."

"I don't."

The room was so quiet I could hear chewing.

"Jett," Bobby said. "We're just looking out for you. If

114

this guy's bad news, we can get rid of him."

"Why? Because I can't keep a partner alive?"

"Just forget it," Bobby said. "Forget it."

They all went back to their food, pretending I wasn't there. I gathered my trash, the remains of my unfinished meal, and slam dunked them into the garbage can.

"The Kid's my partner," I said. "Just back off. You don't know what you're talking about."

And then Bobby was off his chair and coming at me. He took me by the front of my shirt and put me against the wall. The whites of his eyes swelled. I couldn't get my hands up to protect myself, so I held on as best I could.

But everyone was up, and guys wedged between us.

"Knock it off...Knock it off."

Just as quickly as it started, it was over. Bobby was away from me without a punch being thrown. He still looked pissed, and he pointed at me.

"Vince was my friend, too," he said. "We all knew him. We all worked with him."

"You sound like my wife."

I went out of the room, but I heard him talking behind me.

"He was a better man than you. A better man than you by far."

SIXTEEN

When we went back to work after lunch, the Kid told me we had to leave early. I asked him why, but he remained vague.

"Remember that project I was working on at lunch? It's on. And you need to come with me."

"Where?"

"Let's just cut out an hour early. And all will be revealed."

After my run-in in the lunchroom, I didn't have anyone else to fall back on. The Kid was all I had. "Okay," I said. "You can explain on the way."

*   *   *

Ned didn't want to let me go early.

"I told you we have to get caught up," he said, "and you want to take time off?"

"I'll make it up."

He looked around me to where the Kid stood waiting. He lowered his voice.

"What the hell's going on around here?" he said. "I can understand if you're leaving early because you've got a sick kid or something, but you're going off with this guy? What gives?"

Ned had a thin line of perspiration on his upper lip.

"I'll come in early on Monday," I said. "Just let it go."

"I heard you had some kind of dust-up at lunch. You and Bobby. I heard you were fighting over your partner. If he's trouble, Jett, he's gone. I don't care. We have too much work to do."

I had one foot out the door.

"You'll understand in good time," I told him.

And I hoped I was right. For the time being, I had no idea what I was getting myself into.

*   *   *

We went in my car.

The Kid told me to head in the direction of the interstate, going north, and I did. But once we started cruising, I asked the Kid what this was all about.

He didn't answer right away. He sat in the passenger seat, his eyes straight ahead. He rubbed his chin like a wise man. "Remember that first day we worked together," he said, "and you told me about hearing a baby crying in the city?"

"I remember you told me I was full of shit."

The Kid nodded. "That's right, I did, but I didn't stop thinking about what you told me that day. And I started looking into it."

"How?"

"I started with some guys in the army, the ones who guard the gates and patrol the city. I wanted to know if they had heard any of the stuff you heard."

He stopped. He wanted me to egg him on, to beg him for the information. He had me pretty well hooked, so I indulged him. "And?"

He scratched at his chin again. I wondered if he tried that move at home, in front of a mirror. "The higher-ups don't want to admit to anything. The brass. They're all buttoned down and on message. They say that everything's out in the open. What we hear on the news and read in the papers is true. What the government says about the City People is right on the money. No secrets, no lies."

I changed lanes to get around a slow-moving truck. "But…"

"Just keep going. We've got a little ways to go."

"Fine. What else did you hear?"

"Some of the grunts tell a different story," the Kid said. "They've heard things, seen things. Voices… shouts…laughing…crying."

"And what did they see?" I had to force myself to keep my eyes on the road.

"Some of the same shit we've seen. You want to take this exit up here then go left."

"What shit?"

"Traps, attempts to trap their men. Say they're down there on patrol, and they hear a baby crying. What's a soldier supposed to do? Ignore the crying baby?"

I went down the exit ramp and took a left turn at a stop sign. We were out in one of the nicer suburbs. Out there, the trees looked greener, the grass grew thicker. We didn't pass houses full of broken windows, and trash didn't blow through the streets like autumn leaves. We passed the campus of a small, liberal arts college, a collection of ivy-covered limestone buildings founded in the 1880s. I used to fantasize about Sophie going to a place like that, but the more time passed, the farther in the rearview mirror that dream slipped.

The Kid went on with his story. "So they send guys to look, right? And what happens? Ambush. Overrun by

118

City People."

"Christ."

"They've lost maybe ten, fifteen guys that way."

"I've never heard of that happening."

"Of course not." We came to a stop sign, and he pointed right. We drove past a small park with a statue of President Grant, riding a horse, his sword raised for battle. He was facing north, away from the city. Wrong direction, I wanted to tell him. "You think the government wants a story like that getting out? Soldiers getting ambushed by City People who are supposed to be brainless and speechless? How would that look?"

"Why don't they go wipe them out?" I said. "Fuck it."

"Not enough good men left in the army, I guess. It would cost a certain amount of money, lives would be lost. And then the story would get out. The press would see the troop movements, the casualties. Everybody's just hoping the City People die out before they make too much trouble. This is it. Turn left."

We went down a narrow, tree-lined street. The houses were two and three stories tall and built back before World War Two.

"What are we doing here?" I asked.

The Kid consulted a scrap of paper. "That's it, number 789. Pull over there, the white one."

I stopped. The house looked nondescript from the outside. The grass was a little too high, and three newspapers littered the porch. But I didn't concentrate on the house long. Something occurred to me. "Wait a minute," I said. "The government and the army know all this about the City People. They know they're showing signs of intelligence and organization and—"

"And they still send us in there," the Kid said. "And they tell us it's safe during the day."

"It is, though, isn't it?"

"How do we know? How do we know what's true? Think about it, Chief. Do you ever *really* feel safe in there?"

I felt like something had been pulled out from under me, like my body had become weightless. "Fuck, they've been lying to us all along. And Vince..."

"Welcome to the life of a foot soldier, Chief. We're all disposable." He drew the word out, and it rattled around in my head long after he said it. The Kid pointed at the house. "I've been doing some research on my own. Chat rooms and websites. There's a lot of stuff out there about the City People. Crazy shit. The guy who lives here is one of the top researchers on the whole subject, and he said we could come by."

I must have nodded because the Kid opened his door. I didn't move right away. "You all right? You look a little green around the gills."

"I'll be okay."

"Thrown for a little loop?"

"Yeah."

"Your bosses don't give a shit what happens to you out there," the Kid said. "You're just cannon fodder. As long as the machine rocks on, nobody cares who gets eaten up by it."

"I'm going to kill Ned."

The Kid shook his head. "He's just a cog. Shit flows downhill. Somebody shits on his head, he shits on yours. That's the circle of life."

"Still..."

"Hey, you really want to be thrown for a loop?" the Kid said.

I didn't. But I asked the Kid what he was talking about anyway.

"You heard a crying baby, and so did those soldiers."

"Yeah?"

"That means you're not crazy. It means what you thought you heard is really there. You're not off the rails."

"I don't know if that makes me feel better or not," I said. "Do I want to be a sane man in a crazy world?"

"Come on inside here," the Kid said. "We'll put a few more kinks in your brain."

* * *

We went around to the back door. I saw the remains of a vegetable garden, along with rusted porch furniture. A table and three chairs. I couldn't help it. I thought of its value in scrap. That's how far into my brain the job had seeped.

The Kid knocked then whispered to me. "This guy's a little paranoid. He used to teach at the college, but he knows his stuff."

We waited. The Kid knocked again.

The window curtain moved, then someone started undoing a series of locks. I knew that crime had leaked out here, and even these homeowners lived in fear now.

The door opened partway.

A man with a halo of white cottony hair stuck his head out. His face was deeply lined and bearded. His sunken eyes and gaunt frame made him look like an Old Testament prophet, one who had been in the desert for far too many years. "Just you two?" he asked.

"Just like I said," the Kid said.

He didn't invite us in, but stepped back, leaving the door open. The Kid went in like he belonged there, and I followed.

We stepped into a large kitchen. It smelled like cooked onions. The man went through a doorway, and we followed. He led us down a hall and into a crowded study. The blinds were drawn, and every available surface—tables, chairs, floor, window ledges—was covered with books and newspapers.

"Just move that stuff off those chairs," he said.

The Kid moved a bundle of newspapers off a small chair and sat down. I opted for standing.

The man went behind his desk where a computer screen flickered and took a seat. He lifted a set of half-moon glasses to his eyes and stared at the screen. I looked at the Kid. *Why are we here?*

The Kid made a gesture—hands out, palms down—that said *relax*. I didn't think that was possible, so I cleared my throat.

"Hold your horses," the man said. His voice was deep and sonorous, and it was easy to imagine it ringing out in a university lecture hall. His eyes moved across the screen for a few more moments, then he clucked his tongue, removed his glasses and looked at us. "What can I do for you gentleman?"

"I sent you that email about the City People, Mister O'Neill—"

"That's *Doctor* O'Neill. I may have been fired by that college, but I'm still a doctor."

"Right. Sorry." The Kid actually looked chastened. Maybe he was flashing back to his days as an out of control youth, one who spent more than a fair share of his time in the Vice-Principal's office. "We work for the city, both of us."

"Doing what?"

"We collect abandoned cars for the scrap metal," I said.

"Ah. Scrap metal. Feeding the giant maw of the war machine. How nice."

"Excuse me?"

"I know you're just following orders. You're just trying to stay out of trouble and feed your family, right?"

"You don't know anything about me."

The Kid raised his hand, thrust into the unfamiliar role of peacemaker. "The point is," he said, "Jett here —"

"No names," O'Neill said. "Everything I do is monitored. Unless you want the government knocking on your door as well, it's best if we keep your names out of this."

"Are you serious?" I said.

"Very." He made a twirling gesture with his hand. *Hurry up.*

The Kid continued. "My friend and me have worked in the city, and we've seen and heard some things from the City People. Things we thought they couldn't do."

"Things we were told they couldn't do," I said.

O'Neill looked at me and nodded. His gesture carried a hint of approval.

"Right," the Kid said. "And I know some guys in the army, guys who patrol the city, who have seen and heard the same things."

"You have a military bearing," O'Neill said. "Were you in the service?"

"Yes, sir. I just came back."

I expected O'Neill to offer some criticism, but he just nodded, solemn as an undertaker. "Go on," he said. "What phenomena have you observed?"

The Kid looked at me and nodded, so I gave O'Neill the rundown of everything that had happened. The crying baby, the cars in the alley. The Trojan Horse. When I told him about that, his eyes widened, and he scribbled something on a piece of scrap paper. I didn't stop talking though. I even gave him an abridged account of Vince's death. While I related that, he started to nod, and a light of recognition dawned in his eyes.

"I heard about this. It was in the paper."

"That's right."

"So you've seen the City People up close, face to face as it were?"

"I have," I said. "We both have actually. Just today we had a run-in."

"Fascinating. I'd love to have that chance."

"Ride with us some time," the Kid said.

O'Neill tapped his glasses against his thigh. "No, that's not for me. I'm strictly on the sidelines, where it's supposed to be safe. But let me tell you what I've discovered through my research into this matter."

"Sweet." The Kid rubbed his hands together.

O'Neill's eyes settled on the Kid. They were like spotlights, fixing on and illuminating the dark shadows of ignorance. "This isn't a joke," he said. "Or a video game. I've devoted my life to this. My research cost me my job." He turned his eyes on me. "Do you think the government likes having people expose their lies?"

"I suppose they don't take kindly to it."

"You bet your ass they don't. Needless to say, the information I share with you is sensitive and can't be attributed to me in any way. I'm only willing to share this information with you because of your unique proximity to the city. And because I'm beginning to doubt whether my research will ever actually amount to anything. I'm getting to the point where it seems better and nobler to send the information out in any way possible. That's why I've been visiting these chat rooms and websites. It feels like slumming to me, but I feel compelled to get the word out." He let out a deep breath. "It used to be a beautiful world, didn't it? A beautiful world indeed."

SEVENTEEN

O'Neill leaned back in his chair and steepled his fingers in front of his chest. "What do you think caused the City People to be the way they are?" he asked.

The Kid and I looked at each other. I spoke up first. "It's the drinking water. Their drinking water supply was contaminated."

"Terrorists did it," the Kid added. "It's all part of the war."

O'Neill laughed. "Oh, that's rich. You are good little boys, aren't you? Believing every lie they spoon feed you, then going off like little worker bees for the government." He put his finger in his ear and dug around. "This is going to be tougher than I thought."

I looked at the Kid again. "Do we need to sit here and listen to this?" I said. "Let's get out of here."

"Wait." The Kid held up his finger and looked at O'Neill. "I came out here to get the story from you. We left work early. Now don't fuck with us."

O'Neill's face became serious. He took a deep swallow. The Kid had a gift for persuasion. "Okay," O'Neill said, clearing his throat. "I used to teach political science over at the college. One of my areas of expertise was in conspiracies and secret histories. The stories behind the stories. The stories the government doesn't want you to know."

"Like who killed JFK," the Kid said. "That kind of stuff."

O'Neill waved his hand in the air like he was chasing a fly. "Child's play compared to this."

"So then what's the story?" I said. "You obviously know something. What is it?"

"I don't *know* anything for certain." He steepled his fingers again. "No one wants to go on record with this, so everything we know is based on anonymous sources, hypothesis, and speculation. But I believe there's an accumulation of evidence that shows that the City People weren't sickened by a terrorist attack, but by the actions of our own government."

For the second time in the span of twenty minutes, I felt as though gravity had abandoned me. I looked over at the Kid, expecting to see outrage on his face, but he was leaning forward, grinning and nodding. He stared at O'Neill like he was the most fascinating thing in the world.

"That's right," the Kid said. "That's what I'm talking about. I told you, Jett, I told you this guy had the goods."

"I haven't heard anything yet," I said. "Anybody can say something like that, something outrageous. In fact, lots of people do. Where is the evidence?"

"It's all right here." O'Neill clicked something on his keyboard and his computer chimed.

"The internet? That's your source? Are you serious?"

O'Neill turned his withering glance on me. I held his gaze, refusing to look away. "Mr. Dormer," he said, "this isn't the kind of story that the conventional news media will cover and tell the truth about. Our media has basically become an arm of our government. Look at the story of your attack. And yes, I do remember your name from when it was splashed all over the headlines. Do you think the media depicted that accurately?"

"I haven't read about it. I was there."

"The accounts were used to further the government's agenda. It demonized the City People with the express purpose of making people more afraid. It made your partner sound like an innocent victim, a family man struck down by the forces of evil."

"That's one way to look at it."

O'Neill smirked. He looked like someone who knew a secret. "Do either of you remember Project Groundwater?" he said.

I didn't know what he was talking about, but the Kid nodded. "Of course. We were trying to protect ourselves against terrorist attacks on our drinking water."

"And apparently it was rather unsuccessful, since we experienced a so-called terrorist attack, right? The one that caused the City People to turn into who or whatever they are?"

"Right," the Kid said.

"Doesn't it seem odd that we've never found the people responsible for that attack? Despite all of our efforts, the parties responsible are still at large in the world and free to strike again if they so desire?" O'Neill didn't give us a chance to respond. He went on with his theories. "Do you remember the condition of our fair city before that attack?"

"It was a pit," the Kid said. "Crime, drugs. Nobody decent lived down there. Hell, those terrorists did —"

"They did us a favor wiping it off the map," O'Neill said, finishing the Kid's sentence for him. "In one fell swoop, the problem of the cities that had been plaguing America for so many years was taken care of. Wait for the City People to die off, and we take the city back."

"You're saying we did this to our own people?" I asked.

"There's substantial evidence to support that, yes."

"He's fucking-A-right, Jett," the Kid said. "Look at the way they treat us. Sending us in there to face those things."

"Sending you to war," O'Neill said, nodding his head toward the Kid.

"My fucking leg," the Kid said.

I waved my arms back and forth, like an umpire signaling safe. "I don't care about any of this," I said. "With all due respect, Professor, I just don't give a shit. It doesn't matter to me what the government did or didn't do. I'm only interested in one thing, and it isn't conspiracy theories, so I'm sorry we're wasting your time. I'm trying to find my partner."

"You should care," O'Neill said. He looked over at the Kid, and the Kid nodded, and then O'Neill looked back at me.

"What?" I said.

"I know what you're trying to do in there," O'Neill said. "I know you want your partner's body back."

I looked at the Kid, who didn't appear apologetic at all.

"I'm sorry, Jett, but I had to tell him everything or he wouldn't see us."

For a long moment, the three of us stood in silence. Something else chimed on O'Neill's computer, an indication that he had received an email. But he didn't move his eyes to the screen or acknowledge it in any way. Instead, he sat waiting for me to say something, and it was obvious to everyone in the room that the next move was mine.

"Okay," I said. "Tell me what this means to me."

O'Neill nodded, and now I was the difficult pupil

who had finally realized the wisdom of sitting at the feet of the master, the better to learn my lesson from him. "These phenomena, these behaviors you've noticed from the so-called City People have been observed by others. Army personnel. Utility workers. They've noticed behavior that is becoming more organized, more systematic."

Despite my reservations, I nodded. "I've felt a few times that there was an...well, an *intelligence* at work there."

"Exactly," O'Neill said. "And the web is full of this information. People record their encounters with the City People, they talk about them, they analyze them. There's a whole history of the City People being written on the web, free of the intrusion and influence of the government that corrupts and controls the mainstream media." His voice rose with excitement, and his eyes widened as he spoke. "And they're telling a story that is very different from the one the government would have us believe. In this story," he pointed at the computer, "not all of the so-called City People are mindless, shambling monsters bent on devouring us, but some of them are living, thinking beings. They're becoming a society unto themselves."

"With children..." I said. "They're reproducing."

"Exactly," O'Neill said. "We were told they couldn't reproduce. Hell, the government thought they couldn't. But people are hearing babies crying down there. One guy, a National Guardsmen...just hold on a minute."

O'Neill stood up and went to a file cabinet in the corner of the room. I waited patiently, but the Kid stood up and followed him. While O'Neill opened a drawer and paged through its contents, the Kid looked back at me, his head bobbing like a rooster's.

See, I told you so, his gesture said.

O'Neill lifted out what appeared to be an eight by ten photograph. He moved toward me with the Kid following, presumably so we could both see it at once.

"This was taken with a camera phone, so the quality leaves something to be desired. It's been blown up and enhanced by a colleague of mine, a person sympathetic to my work."

He held the photo in his hands while the Kid and I stood on either side.

"What do you see?" O'Neill said.

The image was dark and somewhat blurred. I studied it for a minute, waiting for something to resolve. It was coming into focus for me when the Kid started tapping the center of the photo.

"Right there," he said. "That's it. Do you see it, Jett?"

I did. A small figure stood in the center of the photograph. It resembled a small child, a toddler, its arms swinging up in the air as if he — and it looked like a boy to me — were running or walking fast. The child looked carefree and rather normal.

"What are you saying about this?" I said.

"Look over here." O'Neill ticked his finger against the upper right hand corner of the photo. "Do you see that?"

Again, it was tough to see. There appeared to be a brick wall that the child was walking in front of, and the wall had large letters blocked out on its side. I made out a D, an I and a U.

"That's the stadium," I said. "Down by the river, where the Wolves used to play." A wave of nostalgia passed over me, and I could smell the grass, the spilled beer, the hot dogs and the peanuts. "I used to go there all the time when I was a kid."

O'Neill tapped the picture again, his finger landing right on the child's image.

"This picture was taken just four months ago," he said. "And given the child's age, it's obvious that he was born down there, since the attack. This child was born of the City People."

* * *

O'Neill announced that he needed a drink. He led us out of the cramped study, back through the kitchen and into his dining room. The curtains were drawn there too, and outside the sun was going down, casting a diffuse and rosy light onto the hardwood floor. O'Neill switched on a lamp. He pointed to a collection of liquor bottles and dusty glasses on the antique sideboard.

"Help yourselves," he said. He poured scotch into one of the glasses for himself then looked at the Kid and me.

I went over and poured myself some bourbon. "Kid?"

"I don't drink."

"Never?"

"Never."

He looked serious. I shrugged. "Learn something new every day," I said.

"A brave man to face this world without alcohol," O'Neill said. "Sometimes I think that if anyone wanted to understand my work, or me, and I mean really understand it after I'm gone, all they'd have to do is examine my bar." He patted the lid of the ice bucket. "This is where my most important thoughts come from."

"That's an odd thing to say," I said.

"I'm an odd fellow."

He took a long swallow of his own drink and refilled it. He took the glass to one of the dining room chairs and sat down. The Kid sat down opposite him, and I took a chair at the head of the table. The Kid started drumming his fingers on the tabletop.

I took two long drinks from my glass of bourbon. I wasn't even sure what I felt anymore. O'Neill's information was like having a ton of bricks dropped on my head. The alcohol wasn't going to help me process it, but it might make it a little less bothersome.

"Why do you think the City People are trying to get out?" I said. "Why hide in the trunks of cars and risk their lives to get out of the city?"

"Would you remain in that urban wasteland if you were them?"

"Is it that simple?" I said. "Just escape?"

A police car screamed by outside, its blue lights strobing past the windows. O'Neill rubbed at his beard. "Some people speculate that they want to get out and start a society of their own. Others think they want to make war upon us. We're distracted enough with the war overseas. We're not exactly at full strength back here. You're not the first to notice them trying to escape, although the car is a new angle, one I haven't heard reported yet."

"I need to know the bottom line here," I said. "What does all of this have to do with me and trying to find my partner's body?"

"It's simple, really. You think he's dead, either devoured by the City People, or else turned into one of them through close contact. A bite or something." O'Neill laughed bitterly. "I can't believe I'm having such a conversation. At one time, I would have thought this talk beneath me." He rubbed at his forehead. "You see, you're thinking of the City People in this crude, reactionary manner, and in the process you underestimate them." He leaned forward and pointed at my chest. "The City People aren't what you think they are. If you keep looking, you have no idea what you're going to find."

"You're saying they might be…more like us," the Kid said.

"Exactly," O'Neill said. "And how are you going to deal with that, Mr. Dormer?"

"I don't know." I took another sip of the bourbon. "I don't even know if I'm going to find Vince, or anything else for that matter. All these things you're telling us…it seems impossible, a needle in a haystack, and a lethal haystack to boot."

"Come on," O'Neill said. "I don't doubt you can find him if you want to."

"He's right, Jett," the Kid said, ever the simplifier. "It's easy."

"Easy? If it was so easy, wouldn't we have already found him?"

"Sure," O'Neill said. He had the photograph of the child with him, and he slid it across the table at me. "Everybody knows where most of them congregate."

It was fairly common knowledge that a large number of City People occupied the old baseball stadium by the river. It only made sense. There was a great deal of room, there was cover. When I still read the newspaper, they ran a story about this very issue, and our mayor and the governor called it a disgrace to have such a meaningful piece of our city's history overtaken by beings who only wanted to trash it.

"I get the feeling you want something from me," I said to O'Neill. "I get the feeling you're not just telling us this out of the goodness of your heart."

O'Neill stood up and went to the bar again. "You're right. I do want something." He filled his glass then held out the bourbon to me. I nodded, and he poured a shot into my glass. "I may have been terminated, but I still fancy myself a researcher. I have a scholar's interest in what happens in the city."

He came back to the table and sat down.

"You want us to go in there and report back to you about what we see," I said.

He raised his glass in a mock toast. "You catch on fast. A plus."

But the Kid glared at O'Neill, his eyes like lasers slicing into the Professor's skull. "So *you* want to use us, too? Just like everybody else?"

For his part, O'Neill didn't flinch. He didn't react at all. He continued to stare into his glass as if all the secrets of the world swam at the bottom of his scotch.

"Easy," I said to the Kid. "Easy."

"You're not falling for this, are you?"

"I thought you wanted to go," I said. "Revenge, remember? You brought me here."

"Not to be somebody's patsy."

"Wait," I said. "If he wants us to do this, there has to be something for us. Right?" O'Neill didn't respond, so I said it again. "Right?"

O'Neill finally nodded. "I can get you in," he said.

"Get us in?" the Kid said. "We can get in every day. We work there."

"I can get you in at night," O'Neill said.

"At night? When they're all awake and moving around?" The Kid looked at me. "Is he going to tie us to a telephone pole to make it easy for them to get us?"

O'Neill continued in his calm, lecturing voice. "At night, you're right, they do move around. They're nocturnal. We've been told that they only can come out at night, but that isn't strictly true. They've been seen more and more during daylight hours. It may just be a ploy on their part. Make us think they don't come out during the day. After all, when does the army patrol the city? When do you work there?"

134

He obviously wanted an answer, so I gave him one. "During the day."

"Makes sense they wouldn't be seen much then, right?" We didn't respond, so he kept going. "The information I have indicates that they use the stadium as some kind of base of operations, a headquarters for whatever they do."

"And what exactly do they do?" I said.

"The same thing anybody does. They look for food. They fuck. They look at the stars and moon and say to themselves, *How the fuck did I get so screwed?* They live their lives."

"Sounds like my life," the Kid said. "Except for the fucking part."

I had to laugh. O'Neill grinned like a withered jack-o-lantern. "I bet your partner's in the stadium," he said. "I bet he's right there."

EIGHTEEN

When I pulled into the work parking lot to drop the Kid off, the sun was long gone, the air cooling. A few stars appeared, lonely and distant. The Kid sat with his hand on the door handle. "I'm going to look up some more information tonight," he said. "Maybe talk to more of those army guys. I want to make sure everything jibes."

The parking lot was deserted, the shed quiet.

"I'm not sure we have any choice but to trust O'Neill," I said. "He's given us the information we need. We'd be fools not to use it."

"You're willing to go in there at night? And go down to the stadium?"

I thought about that precipice that I associated with the Kid, the one I stood at the edge of and looked over. I was ready to jump. "Yeah," I said. "I don't know much about anything. But when we were there talking to the nutty professor, I decided I'm in this for the long haul, come hell or high water. I can't turn back."

The Kid held his hand out in the space between us, and we shook. "Now that's the chief we used to sing about around the campfire," he said.

"I'm coming in early tomorrow and telling Ned about yesterday," I said. "These guys deserve to know."

The Kid nodded reluctantly. "Okay," he said.

"I think we can use this information to our advantage," I said. "O'Neill wanted us to call him tomorrow, so I'll come by your place in the morning. After I'm done with Ned."

He smiled then slipped out the door and into the night.

*   *   *

Our house was dark when I arrived home. I knew Sophie was long asleep.

I moved through the house like a ghost, checking the locks, and undressed in the bathroom so as not to disturb Nicole. In what had become an all too-familiar routine, I slid into the bed next to her, being careful not to steal too many of the covers. We shared the bed like strangers, beached together by circumstance.

"I guess I should ask what you were doing," she said.

"Work stuff."

"This late?"

She kept her back to me. Her voice was faint in the darkness.

"I might be working some more late nights," I said. "Some things are changing down there."

"Changing so that you're working at night?"

I didn't respond.

"When you didn't come home at the regular time, I called my mom. I didn't give her any details, but I said Sophie and I might come and visit for awhile."

"Oh?"

"Yes." She rolled over a little so that we were closer to each other. "I don't have to go. But I will if you keep acting this way."

I closed my eyes and pictured Sophie. Her laugh, her big eyes. Her silly grin and language of gibberish. "I wish you wouldn't. If you would just be patient, this could all be over soon. Real soon."

She rolled back into her original position. "You and I have both seen what being a widow has done to Marie," she said. "I don't want to go down that road. And I'm not going to do it to Sophie. She's my light. She used to be yours."

"Nicole, please. Just wait."

Even in the darkness, I could tell she was shaking her head. "I've been waiting, Jett. I can't wait any more." She sniffled. "It's your choice, though. I just want you to know that you're the one making the decisions for all three of us."

"It's not that simple," I said.

"It might be, if you would just talk to me about it. Hell, you don't have to talk to me. Just talk to someone."

"I'm handling this the best way possible," I said, my voice slightly too loud in the darkness. "I really think this is the way it has to be."

*   *   *

In the space between Nicole and I, something moved. A small, squirming presence on top of the sheets. We never, ever let Sophie sleep in the bed with us. Too dangerous, we both figured, too much of a risk of one of us rolling on top of her. But occasionally, Nicole let Sophie fall asleep between us before moving her to the nursery. I didn't remember Sophie being there, but we all must have fallen asleep, leaving the baby in the bed with us.

I sat up. "Nicole?" I whispered.

She had her back to me, and she didn't respond.

"Nicole?"

My eyes were fully adjusted to the dark. Sophie was on top of the comforter, her face toward Nicole's side of the bed. She squirmed, her feet digging for purchase against the bedclothes. Lately, she had been crawling more and more, and it was getting to be an effort for the two of us to keep up with her when she was down on the floor. I feared that she might crawl off the edge of the bed if she got going, so I reached down and picked her up.

"Sophie, you're freezing," I said.

We had left her to sleep on top of the blankets, an idiot mistake. I pulled her close to me and kissed her on top of her head. "Are you sick, honey?"

I gathered up the covers and swaddled them around her, hoping to warm her up. Not only was I the world's worst friend, but I now qualified as one of the world's two worst parents for allowing my daughter to sleep in a cold house without blankets.

I sat like that, rocking Sophie and hoping my body heat would transfer over to her. After a few minutes, I looked down to see if she was asleep. She wasn't. Her eyes were open wide, and even in the darkness, I could see that she wasn't just pale from sickness, but rather her skin carried the pallor of the grave. Her mouth was slack, her eyes unfocused. But she still breathed. I had just seen her moving.

"Oh, Jesus," I said. "Sweet God."

She was one of them. My sweet, innocent baby girl was a City Person.

"Nicole! Nicole!"

I fumbled out of the covers and stood up next to the bed, still holding the baby in my hands.

Nicole stirred on her side of the bed. She rolled over and looked at me, the anger in her eyes apparent even in the dark.

"It's you," she said. "You brought that here."

"No."

"You did," she said, rolling back over as if it were any normal morning. "You brought that shit here."

"No, no…"

I didn't know what else to do. I wanted out of that room. I needed to call a doctor. I took a few steps, Sophie still clutched in my arms, and saw a figure in the doorway… indistinct, shadowy.

I froze.

It stepped forward and the face became visible.

"Vince," I said, but there was no joy in seeing my old friend. He'd done this. He'd infected my baby. "What have you done, Vince? Why would you do this to her, how — how could you do this?"

"We should check out a Wolves' game down at the old stadium," he said. "We had some good times there."

"Sophie's sick. My little girl, she's…"

Vince looked down at the baby in my arms as if seeing her for the first time. He regarded her with all the interest one would grant to a bag of groceries. "You can take care of that," he said.

"How? Tell me how."

"You know."

"No, I don't."

"You've been doing it enough lately." Vince laughed bitterly. "You know, in the city, with your new partner."

"No." I shook my head. "I wouldn't do that."

"You seem to think it's the only way. You've become quite adept at it."

"But not Sophie…"

And then, as if she'd been slicked down with cooking oil, the baby slipped from my hands, a slow-motion drop to the floor. She landed with the most sickening thump I have ever heard in my life, one that reverberated in my brain like the blast from a cannon, and her head, her small precious head, liquefied on contact with the floor into the soupy, gray mush that I had seen coming from the crushed remains of the City People. It splattered on my bare feet and legs, a nauseating cold goop.

I looked up at Vince.

He smiled at me. "So...how about that Wolves' game?"

And then I was suddenly sitting up in bed.

The alarm hadn't rung. I looked over, hoping I hadn't disturbed Nicole again. She was turned on her side, her usual sleeping position, one arm tucked underneath her, the other gripping a spare pillow. Her breathing came steady and regular.

I slipped out of bed, my movements as stealthy as a burglar's, and went to Sophie's room. She was in her crib, asleep, her small right fist clutching a pink blanket. The mobile above her crib had long ago run down, a victim of entropy.

I checked the locks on both windows. They were tight as a drum, but still, I wondered if we shouldn't add bars to the windows as so many of our neighbors had done. I questioned whether any place was safe any more. Between O'Neill and the City People and my own dreams, I felt like I lived in the world's last protected fortress. And the walls were about to spring leaks.

I went back to the crib. I resisted the urge to reach in and touch her. I didn't want to wake her up and throw the morning into chaos before it needed to be there.

"You're up early."

I turned to see Nicole in the doorway, her eyes still puffy from sleep.

"I don't want to wake her," I said. "Or you."

"She'll be up soon enough."

I looked back down into the crib, back at my

daughter.

"Did you say why you're up so early?" Nicole said.

"I have to go talk to Ned about some things."

"What things?"

Her voice carried a trace of hope, and I found it hard to believe that she could still feel that emotion for me, someone who had let her down so many times. I couldn't look at her. "Just some things about work. Arrangements with my schedule. I told you I might be working nights."

She inhaled a quick, short breath. She might as well have been surrendering.

I turned from the crib and came to the door where Nicole stood. She didn't move out of my way at first, so I stopped.

"I won't be here when you get back," she said. "Remember?"

"I remember," I said. "And I'd be disappointed in you if you stayed, I guess. I married you because you were strong, because you always do what you say you're going to do."

Nicole's eyes filled with tears, and before I changed my mind, I slipped past her, my body brushing against hers in the doorway. At the end of the hall, I stopped and looked back.

"Take care of our girl for me," I said.

"I will."

"And wherever you go, your mom's place or somewhere else, will you do me a favor? Will you be careful? Will you just be as careful as you can possibly be?"

"I will, Jett. I promise. Will you be careful, too? For us?"

I nodded. "I'll do my best."

And then I left my life with them behind in favor of a new one.

NINETEEN

The shed was quiet when I arrived that morning.

Most of the drivers hadn't shown up yet, and only the mechanics were busy inside, prepping the rigs for the coming day of work. Outside, the crusher pounded on and on, compacting the vehicles into manageable bundles that would later be hauled away on flatbed trucks. I wondered how many City People had surrendered their lives to the crusher. But the follow-up thought was even more disturbing: how many had made it to freedom?

Ned stood in front of the snack machine in the break room, staring through the glass at the endless variety of selections. He held loose change in his hand, and he jingled it as he looked, giving off the air of a man who, presented with so many options, just couldn't make a decision.

"Ned."

He stopped shaking the change and turned toward the sound of my voice. "Hi, Jett. I didn't get breakfast this morning."

"Can I talk to you?"

"Sure." He must have heard an edge in my voice. His

eyes started darting nervously left and right. "What's on your mind?"

"In your office." I made sure it didn't come out as a question.

Ned followed me in, and I closed the door. He had a candy bar in his hand, which he tossed on the desk. "You seem a little fired up, Jett."

"I have a right to be, don't I?"

"How's that?"

"Every man working here has a right to be, especially the drivers."

"I don't follow."

"How long have you known about the City People?"

"I'm sorry. I don't—"

"Damn it, Ned. Do not fuck with me. You know what I mean."

Ned tried to hold my gaze, but his eyes slid off of mine and down to the floor. He took a deep swallow and let his body plop back into his desk chair. He still didn't say anything.

"You've been sending us out, knowing it's more dangerous than everybody lets on. You've been hanging our asses out to dry. And…Jesus…Vince…Vince died because of it."

"Now Jett—"

"You have blood on your hands," I said, pointing at him. "You have blood all over you."

Ned started blubbering. He held his hands up in front of his body, as if he thought I was going to hit him. He said the word no over and over. It took me a moment to realize he wanted me to see his hands, to know that there wasn't any blood there. He looked so pathetic, so fat and helpless, that I felt a sliver of pity for him. My anger went down a few degrees. "I'm sorry," he said. "I'm sorry." Tears and snot merged on his face. He had a box of kleenex on the corner of his desk. I shoved it in his direction.

"Clean yourself the fuck off."

He pulled a fistful of kleenex out of the box and started dabbing at his face. I paced, cooling my heels, while he composed himself with a symphony of sniffles. "It's not my fault, Jett," he said.

"Don't say that," I said. I held my index finger up in the air. "Do *not* say that."

He started nodding, his face obscured by the Kleenex. "You know damn well that it's your fault, damn fucking well."

He continued to nod. "You're right. It is my fault, all my fault. I don't know what's wrong with me."

"Shut up."

"They made me send you guys out. I found out about these reports, but they said to disregard them. They said we needed the scrap, and that the chances of anything happening were slim. Real slim. They knew, though, Jett. The guys at City Hall knew."

"How could you go along?"

"I need this job," he said, his blubbering slowing down. "My mother lives with me, you know. And I have a student loan."

"That's such a load of bullshit."

"When Vince died, I was going to quit. Here, let me show you." He started clicking his mouse. "I've got a draft of my resignation letter right here. I was ready to do it, I swear. Vince was such a good man. A great man."

"So why didn't you quit?"

He sniffled again. "Oh, Jett…"

"Did they force you? Did they threaten you?"

He shook his head. "Interest rates went up. The loan."

"Bullshit."

I pounded my fist on his desk. Ned yelped, and papers and pens flew into the air. The act brought me a measure of calm. My fist stung where it hit the desk, but more of the anger had flowed out of me. "Here's what you're going to do to make it right," I said.

"Of course, of course. Anything."

"You're going to go out there and tell those guys of the danger they're in."

Ned's mouth hung open a little, but he didn't speak.

"Ned?"

"They'll kill me," he said. "Then I'll get fired. But first those guys will kill me."

"Either them or me."

He nodded weakly, the loose flesh under his chin shaking.

"And then you're going to let me and the Kid have the number one rig."

"I already gave it to you."

"I don't mean you're going to let us use it. Listen to what I say. You're going to *give* it to us. For our own personal use."

"I can't do that. It's city property—"

"Ned. I'm running out of patience here. You're going to give us full access to the rig. And you're going to continue to pay my salary, even though I'm not going to be working here any more. No matter what happens, keep paying my salary."

He started to speak, but stopped himself.

"It's for Nicole and Sophie. Hell, keep paying the Kid, too. We'll use his money if we need something. You got that?"

"Sure. Whatever you want." He looked to be contemplating whether or not to say more. He swallowed. "What exactly is it you're doing with the rig?"

"Ned, in this case, the less you know the better."

He looked relieved to be kept out of the loop. "Is there anything else I can do for you?"

I had said all I came to say, so I pointed to the door. "Get your ass out there and sing your song."

*   *   *

I needed to go meet the Kid so that we could plan our next move. I didn't feel any great need to attend Ned's meeting with the drivers. He was cowed enough to do what I had told him, and I needed to take care of my own business right then.

In a way, Vince's death caused a breech, perhaps real, perhaps imaginary, between the other drivers and me. Going back to work was meant to heal that breech, to bring me back into the fraternity that had for so long been central to my identity.

But meeting the Kid had changed all of that. Rather than bringing me back in, it had instead driven me further away. Laying down my cards with Ned ended up being my last act as an employee of the city, and on my way out the door to see the Kid, I grabbed the keys to the number one rig from the lockbox.

When I stepped out into the parking lot, heading for my own car, I saw a figure approaching. At first I thought it was a beggar, one of the many homeless men who wandered the streets around the shed, looking for handouts to buy alcohol and drugs.

But this guy was well-groomed, his head immaculately shaved. It was the cane and the shuffling gait that threw me and made him seem thirty years older than he really was. It was McGruder, hobbled and broken, but attempting to come into work.

"Look at you," I said.

"Jett."

It had been a couple of weeks since his beating, and his voice came out with some effort. I didn't know if I was supposed to help him or wait and let him shuffle along on his own. But even if I did offer assistance, I couldn't imagine what form it would take. So I stood still until he reached me. "Are you coming back to work?" I said.

"Just visiting." He breathed heavily. "I thought it would do me some good to get out and see the guys."

"They're having a meeting."

They, I said, not *we*.

McGruder also noticed my word choice. He cocked his head at me. "Where are you going?"

When he turned his head, the sun hit him straight on, and for the first time, I saw the full extent of his injuries. The skin around his eyes was still purple and yellow, and just above his ear a line of stitches extended several inches. It was rare and surprising to see him without his sunglasses, and it only called more attention to the damage that had been done to his face. He noticed me staring and cleared his throat. "Jett? Where are you going?"

I took my eyes off his injuries, but couldn't bring myself to look at him straight on. "I don't really work here anymore, I guess."

He looked surprised, but not overly surprised. I expected the news to shock him. In a way, I hoped it would. I wanted someone else to mark the moment as a significant turning point in my life as well as in the life of the shed. "What are you going to do?" he said.

"I have something to take care of." I had the keys pressed into my palm, their metal edges digging into my skin. "I can't really talk about it. But when that's done, if it's done, I guess I really don't know. I haven't really thought about what's to come next."

As the words came out, it occurred to me how strange it was to be speaking so frankly with McGruder, a man I had previously viewed as my arch-nemesis. Maybe his beating and my affiliation with the Kid had worked to bring down the barrier that previously existed between us. "I'm not really surprised to see you walk away," he said. "You probably came back too soon."

"It's more complicated than that."

"Isn't everything?"

It was. I had tried to make my life simple—get Vince back—but complications resulting from that choice were as numerous as the stars in the night sky. I couldn't imagine how Ned's meeting was going, but something told me I didn't want to be around for the aftermath. Too many questions would be asked, and again, I'd be diverted off my original course.

I squeezed the keys tighter and resolved to go. "I'm sorry this happened to you," I said.

"Why are you sorry for it?"

"Because I think I know who did it, and I feel responsible. I didn't intend for things to turn out that way. I didn't intend for a lot of things to turn out the way they turned out, actually."

McGruder smiled. His mouth was a thin, tight line. "I know your partner's the one who did me," he said. "I can't prove it, but I know. It just makes sense."

I nodded. "Why haven't you turned him in?"

He adjusted his cane, tightening his grip and shifting his weight from one leg to the other. He grimaced again and took a quick intake of breath. I reached out to steady him, but he shook his head. "I'm fine. I have to go, but I'm fine." He looked steadier, and the pained look passed from his face. "Getting your ass kicked changes your perspective," he said. "I've had a lot of time to think. I've been a prick to a lot of people, and I guess I've had a

149

beating coming for a long time. Maybe this one makes up for all the others I should have had. But I'm just not interested in carrying stuff around with me like that. Being pissed off, taking it out on somebody else. Revenge. Who needs it, right? I'm alive, and that's what matters. It's better to let the rest go. Isn't it?"

I reached out and gave his hand, the one holding the cane, a gentle squeeze. I wanted to let him know that I understood, but the truth was, I just didn't. "It sure would be nice to think so," I said.

TWENTY

The Kid lived in a rundown little building about twenty minutes from work. I had dropped him off before but had never ventured inside. The interior hallway was dingy, and received a sickly, yellow light from a lone sconce mounted on the wall. Behind one of the closed doors, a baby cried, and somebody else's TV played at an ear-splitting volume. The Kid let me into his place when I knocked. He held the phone in his hand.

"O'Neill isn't answering," he said.

The room was small and sparsely furnished. A twin mattress on the floor, a card table pushed against one wall.

"I've tried emailing him, too, but it bounces back." He put the phone down. "I don't like it. He told us to call him in the morning."

"We'll try again later. He does have to leave the house occasionally. He has to eat."

"No way. We've got to go right now." He grabbed a jacket off the mattress. "Let's go."

I retraced, from memory, the route we took to O'Neill's house the day before. I drove, and the Kid chewed at a loose piece of skin near his thumbnail while

I told him about my conversation with Ned. He grunted a couple of times while I talked and only spoke up to ask a question once.

"Why did you take the keys to the rig?" he said.

"I thought we might need it. There's something about that big thing that makes me feel protected."

"True."

"And I thought if we went in after hours a city vehicle might give us some cover."

"Good," the Kid said, his voice approving. "Good thinking."

"You've taught me a little something about being devious."

He didn't smile, and I chose not to tell him about seeing McGruder.

When we pulled up in front of O'Neill's house, the Kid stared through the passenger side window, still chewing on his thumb.

"It's okay," I said. "We'll find him."

"I don't know."

"What?"

"You know that feeling?" he said. "The one I had when we opened that trunk?"

"You're having it now?"

"Yeah. Something's not right. It hasn't been right all day."

"Should we call the police?"

The Kid looked back at me, his face full of disdain. "You're so fucking thick sometimes." He turned away from me, pushed open the door and started for O'Neill's house.

I scrambled to keep up, despite his bad leg. The Kid didn't show any sign of hesitation or caution. He walked to the back of O'Neill's house, with me following behind, as if we were showing up for a Sunday afternoon picnic.

He knocked on the door. Hard.

"O'Neill."

He knocked again.

"Maybe the neighbors saw him," I said.

The Kid ignored me and kept pounding. He reached down and tried the knob. It turned under his pressure, and he pushed the door open. "Come on," he said.

"Why don't we wait in the car?"

But the Kid was already inside. I could hang around in the car or on the porch, or I could go along with him. I followed him inside. The kitchen looked and smelled the same. Fried onions. Nothing looked out of place. "O'Neill?" the Kid called.

No answer again.

We went down the hallway toward the study, but before we arrived there, I saw that the bathroom door was closed. "Kid," I whispered. "Look. Maybe he's in the john."

"O'Neill?" The Kid went to the bathroom door and knocked. "O'Neill? You in there? It smells like he's taking a shit."

No one responded. The house remained silent as a tomb.

The Kid reached down and tried the knob on the bathroom door. It turned.

"O'Neill?" he said. "It's us."

The door squeaked open.

At some point, the weight of the body had caused the shower curtain rod to pull loose from the plaster wall, but not before the bed sheet wrapped around O'Neill's neck choked the life out of him. He lay across the edge of the tub, the top half of his body inside and the lower half outside.

We went to him, and the Kid touched his hand.

"Cold as ice," he said.

The odor of his evacuated bowels hit me then in full-force, and I went to the sink and leaned over it. I gagged, hard, but nothing came up.

The Kid stepped into the tub and pushed the small window open, letting in fresh air. He took me by the arm and pulled me out of the bathroom. "Let's get out of here," he said, pulling the door shut behind us. We went out into the dining room. My eyes were burning, my hands shaking. The Kid looked angry. "I knew it," he said.

"Why? Why did he do it?"

"Fuck him. He let us down."

"I thought he was going to help us."

The Kid grabbed the bottle of scotch off the sideboard and threw it against the wall, where it shattered in a spray of liquor and glass. "Damn it," he said.

He ran his hand through his hair. His face was flushed. It glowed like a hot coal.

"Let's go," I said. "We'll call the police."

"Hold on." He held up his index finger. "Just wait here. I'm going to check the office."

I was in no mood to argue. And I wasn't ready to go back down that hallway. I hoped to leave the house without going back down there at all.

But the Kid's voice shattered that hope.

"Jett," he called. "You've got to get back here. We've got a problem."

* * *

I stopped in the office doorway.

The smell from the bathroom had dissipated, thanks to the open window. The Kid was in O'Neill's office, standing behind his desk. I could see the problem right away.

"The computer's gone," I said.

The Kid opened a file cabinet drawer.

"These are empty, too."

I looked over my shoulder toward the closed bathroom door.

"He didn't do that to himself, did he?" I said.

The Kid ignored me. He pulled open every file cabinet drawer he could find, and then rooted around on the desk and the chairs around the room.

"This is all just junk," he said. "Old exams. Newspapers. Nothing of any value."

"He was right. They were after him."

"Let's go. We'll have to find another way."

We hustled down the hallway and through the kitchen, but something about the whole scene bothered me. I didn't believe that O'Neill would let everything go that easily. He struck me as the kind of guy who was just paranoid enough to have layers of contingency plans in place. "Just a second," I said.

"What?"

We were stopped at the kitchen door.

"O'Neill was a little crazy, wasn't he?"

"Sure."

"But not so crazy that he wouldn't have a backup of everything he did and thought."

"He's been cleaned out. They took everything."

I turned and went into the dining room where we had our drinks. The Kid came along behind me.

"Yesterday when we were here he said that if anyone wanted to understand his work, all they had to do was look in his bar. This is where all his best ideas came from."

"So? He was a drunk and a loon."

I lifted the lid off the ice bucket. It was half full of water from melted ice, perhaps the ice that was there yesterday. I dumped it onto the floor, splashing the Kid's boots.

"Careful," he said.

"I don't think he cares about his carpet anymore."

I felt around on the vinyl sides and bottom of the bucket, scratching at it with my fingernails. Where the bottom met the side, my nail caught on something. A small tear or opening in the lining. I worked at it until I could get a good grip then peeled it back. It came easily, like it was meant to be opened. A metallic silver disc was underneath, a little damp from the seeping water, but otherwise in shining, pristine condition.

I held it up to the Kid, who stared at it with open-mouthed admiration.

A crazy and a loon, yes, but a well-prepared crazy.

"Now we can go."

TWENTY-ONE

The Kid didn't own a computer. I asked him how he went to all of these websites and chat rooms, and he looked at me like I was a simpleton.

"The library, of course," he said.

So we headed for the branch near the Kid's apartment.

"The librarians there love me," he said. "They started fawning all over me the minute they found out I was a veteran."

"How'd they find out?"

"I told them," he said. "They want me to come in and talk to the kids someday about being in the war. Maybe I should tell them about all this stuff. The City People. The scrap metal. O'Neill."

"I think they want to hear about heroes."

"Ain't none of those left," the Kid said. "How did you know where to find that disc, Chief? You went all *Mission Impossible* on me there."

"O'Neill told us when we were there," I said.

"He told us? I don't remember that."

"He didn't tell us directly. But I remember him tapping on that ice bucket. He wanted someone to be able

157

to find that stuff if they did him in."

"You're full of surprises, Chief. Like a box of Crackerjacks."

"Do you think someone killed him because of us? Do you think they know he was starting to talk and did him in?"

"I doubt it," the Kid said. "He was probably on their list for awhile. The fact that they took him down after we talked to him is just a coincidence."

"You really think that?"

We pulled into the library parking lot, among the minivans and family cars.

"Yes. But it can't hurt for us to be careful. We haven't exactly been making friends along the way."

We walked into the library and found ourselves in the middle of children's story hour.

A bespectacled young man in a cardigan sweater read from a picture book to a circle of wide-eyed, open-mouthed kids, ages two to four. They munched cookies and sipped cups of punch while the man told them about a dinosaur who had been separated from his family. The mothers stood at the back of the circle, holding coats and purses, big smiles across their faces as if they had found the world's bright center of happiness.

For a moment, I paused, admiring the scene and its absolute simplicity. I had turned my back on that life just that morning, but its allure remained strong. One phone call and I could have it back.

But didn't these people know there was a war on? Not just overseas, but here at home, on the streets of their city?

The Kid tugged my elbow, bringing me back to the task at hand.

"Back here, Chief," he said in his best library whisper.

I followed him past the circulation desk—where a

middle-aged librarian waved and smiled at the Kid — to a row of computers in the back corner of the library. The Kid sat down and logged on, while I took the seat next to him. I handed the disc over.

He slid it in and started pounding on the keys.

"What if what we're looking for isn't here?" he said.

"It has to be."

"You think this will tell us a way into the city?"

"Do you believe in O'Neill's knowledge?"

"Sure. He's crazy, but he knew his stuff."

"Then it will be there." I looked around. I saw what I needed over by the bathrooms. "I'll be right back."

I went over to the payphone and dug into the pockets of my coveralls, looking for change. I knew this wasn't the best idea in the world, but I had some things to say to Nicole. I wanted to tell her about the money from Ned. And, really, I wanted to hear her voice again, to get a last glimpse of normality. I dialed the familiar number and waited.

While the phone rang, I watched the storyteller. He had laid the book aside and was talking directly to the children, his arms making wide, dramatic circles in the air. The kids cheered and laughed.

The phone kept ringing and ringing. I assumed I had missed them and was about to hang up.

"Hello?"

The sound of Nicole's voice threw me. Again, I thought about hanging up.

"Hello?"

"It's me," I said. "Jett."

"Jett." She sounded out of breath. "Where the hell are you?"

"What's the matter?"

"Jett..." Her voice trailed off. She sniffled. "Ned's been calling here all morning looking for you."

"I talked to him this morning. Everything's fine."

"It's not about you. It's your partner. Are you with him?"

I turned and looked back at the row of computers. The Kid was tapping away, the tip of his tongue pressed between his teeth. "I don't know what he's doing," I said.

"They know you're with him. Don't lie."

Something about the use of the word *they* bothered me. It sent up a red flag.

"Do you mean Ned?"

"Not just Ned. Two men came to our house today, two men from the Army. They weren't in uniform but they had IDs. They're looking for the Kid. He's in trouble, Jett."

"What kind of trouble?"

"They didn't tell me. Ned thinks he did something in the war, something illegal. Those army guys said they want to talk to him about it. A friendly chat, they called it. Jett, they didn't seem very friendly."

"Look, Nic, everything is going to be fine." I looked back at the Kid again. He had moved to the printer, and when he saw me, he gave me a big thumbs up. "I talked to Ned. He's going to pay you my salary for a little while. Take that money and go to your mom's if you want."

"Jett. It's not too late for you to turn back from this. I know you want to do this for Vince, but it's not worth it. Don't give up your life, too."

I turned away from the Kid and faced the telephone. The chrome faceplate with the number pad reflected my image back at me, warpy and distorted. The little kids let out another cheer behind me.

"Just take the money, take Sophie, and go to your mom's. You'll be safe there, far from the city."

"Safe from what?"

"I can't explain now. Just go. If I can get there, I will."

"If, Jett? *If?*" She sounded scared and desperate.

"Yes. If." There was nothing else to say. "Good-bye."

*   *   *

The Kid stood by the printer, a thick sheaf of white paper in his hand.

"We've got it all," he said. "Maps. Checkpoints. Troop movements. It's all here."

I placed my hand on his upper arm and exerted a little pressure.

"We've got to go," I said.

"There's more to print out."

"Do you have what's essential?"

"Yes."

"Then let's go. It's getting hot for us. Too hot."

The Kid collected the disc from the computer's drive, then came along behind me. The librarian wished us a good afternoon, and as we moved toward the door, I saw that the kids, happily ensconced in their fantasy world, were spinning in circles and chanting a rhyme I remembered from my childhood.

Ashes. Ashes. We all fall down.

TWENTY-TWO

We decided it wasn't safe to go to the Kid's apartment. And we couldn't exactly go to my house and drag Nicole and Sophie into all of this.

The Kid suggested the Delta Avenue Park, a sprawling area of trees, benches, and picnic tables not too far from the heart of the city. Families still went there during the day — in fact, we had taken Sophie there the previous summer — and no one would think to look for the two of us there. It helped, too, that we had my car and not the rig, which would advertise our presence to everyone.

We went to a drive-through on the way and picked up food. My guts churned with nervous energy, and I doubted I would be able to eat anything, but the Kid loaded up and insisted I do the same.

"Let's eat and drink," he said, "for tomorrow..."

He left the thought unfinished, but I knew what he meant.

Rather than sit in the car, we took an empty bench on the edge of the park. Delta Avenue ran along a high hillside overlooking the city, offering a panoramic view of the surrounding area. The Kid took large bites of his hamburgers, so that he looked a little like a snake swallowing an entire rat, while I sipped on my coke, wary of taking in anything more substantial.

When he finished and had wiped the last remnants of ketchup and salt from his face with a stained napkin, I reminded him of his promise to tell me why he was in trouble.

"You owe me the story," I said. "What are they after you for?"

He threw the soiled napkin into the empty bag and drank from his own paper cup. "You got it, Chief. No secrets, I know. As soon as you told me that someone was looking for me, I knew what it was."

"Travis Coffey and those guys hinted that you did something in the war, something illegal. Is that what this is all about?"

The Kid put his drink down and let out a loud belch. "I did some things in the war," he said. "Things the government didn't approve of. And that's the shit that's hitting the fan right now, I would reckon. But as far as illegal goes...well, we're sort of into a gray area when we talk about that word, aren't we? Especially considering the things you and I have been doing lately. Right?"

"You've got a point."

"I know I do." He looked away, toward the view of the city, its buildings and streets, its empty highways and bridges. "It looks awfully quiet from up here, doesn't it? You can look at it from this distance and think everything's okay down there, as right as rain."

I couldn't disagree.

"Of course, most things look okay from a distance," he said. "It's only when we get close up that we get to see things the way they really are. That's why I'm glad we've been able to work together like this, Jett."

"Why is that?"

The Kid looked over at me. "Because you've been

able to see the world close up. You can't just stay in your little house and do your little job without thinking of what's really going on."

"I guess you've been my tour guide."

"Somebody had to do it," he said. "One way or another, we all learn the lesson."

* * *

Then the Kid told his story.

"When I was over there, in the war, and before I got my leg blown off, I was assigned to a temporary prison camp. Camp Presto they called it because we were supposed to get these guys in and out fast. Process them, find out what we could, then send them on their way to a more permanent camp. Nothing unusual.

"Except, somebody higher up, some colonel or general, figured out that Camp Presto would be a good place to sort of *lose* prisoners for a little while. Since they came there to be processed, there was always a certain amount of time before the prisoner was actually in the system. A dead period. And this higher-up decided to start earmarking certain prisoners for a *longer* dead period. It was nothing overt, but a guy would come in, and we'd get the word that there was no rush on him. So we wouldn't enter him into the system right away."

"Why did they do this?" I said.

"So they could come and visit these guys, you know what I mean? We'd bring the guy in and not process him, and pretty soon we all noticed that these higher-ups would show up, usually late, sometimes in the middle of the night, and they'd want to see one of those unprocessed prisoners."

"For what?"

"Well, Jett, they didn't want to play cards with them.

I stood guard outside those locked doors. I heard the guys screaming in there. It was like all their dignity was leaving them." He looked away again, back over the city, although I had the feeling he was really seeing something else. "I can still hear those screams. I don't think I'll ever forget them, not until I'm senile and have forgotten everything else. I think those will be the last things to go."

"And you're in trouble now because you worked there?" I said, my voice lower. "A guilt by association thing?"

"I wasn't associated with anything," he said. "I did it. I am guilty, at least in the eyes of the law."

"Of what?"

"Torture. War crimes. Whatever you want to call it." The Kid started laughing. "War crimes. Now that's a funny expression, isn't it Chief? *War crimes.*"

"Okay. So you want me to see things up close," I said. "You don't want me to hide anymore. What exactly did you do over there?"

"What did I do in the war, daddy?" He laughed again. "Imagine if I went into that library and told those kids about this stuff. The little shits would have nightmares for years. Their mommies would be crying their eyes out. They wouldn't be able to go home and watch Doctor Phil or *Guiding Light* after that, would they?" The Kid took another long drink. "As you can imagine, some of those guys we captured were pretty hard. They weren't going to talk or give anything up. Some of them went down right away. There are chickenshits everywhere. But the real hard cases, the real badasses, they couldn't be broken that fast. And why should some colonel with intelligence connections spend a lot of his valuable time trying to break some guy who doesn't want to be broken if there's a steady stream of new victims coming in? Doesn't make sense, does it?"

"I guess it depends on what they think the guy knows."

"Right. So say they have some guy who won't talk, but they still think he might know something. What are they going to do with him?" The Kid looked at me like he wanted an answer. I shook my head. "They try to get us, the guards, to break them. And they let us know that we can use whatever method we want."

"Torture?"

"Except they don't call it torture. They don't even say that we can hurt these guys. They just tell us to get whatever information we can out of them, and they suggest that whoever gets the good information will get promoted. Or better yet, rotated back to the States."

The Kid knew me well. I didn't want to hear the details of what he did over there. In the past, this was the point at which the TV would have been switched off, the radio silenced, the newspaper thrown away. But the Kid had never let me wiggle off the hook. His insistence on being heard forced my eyes and ears open. I couldn't look away.

"What kinds of things did you do?"

"You might find this hard to believe, but at first, I didn't do anything. There were other guys, crazy guys, guys who make me look like Mister Rogers, and they were doing most of the stuff." He cleared his throat. "They would make these guys have sex with each other, make them give each other blow jobs and hand jobs. And they'd take pictures of it all and say they were going to send them to the prisoners' wives and families. I watched those guys do it, I watched those prisoners scream and cry, and I just didn't care. It was a war after all, right? These guys were the enemy. If they weren't in our custody, they'd be trying to blow us up or shoot us."

"Sure."

"The human body and the human psyche can adapt to just about anything. It's like doing drugs or drinking. Eventually, you build up a tolerance and have to find more creative ways to get high. Same goes for torture. The victim adapts, develops a tolerance—physical or mental—and you have to come up with a new way to hurt the person." The Kid looked down at his hands. "Chief, it turns out I have a gift I didn't know I had. I can think of ways to hurt people like it's nobody's business."

I wanted to disagree with him on one point. Grief hurts like nobody's business, and he hadn't created grief.

"We got this guy in there, a real hard case. Nothing we did bothered him. He didn't mind the sex stuff. He seemed to enjoy it. He'd suck another guy's dick and look right at the camera and wave. Beatings didn't hurt him or slow him down. He'd come back for more with a smile on his face. It bugged the shit out of me, Jett. I can't tell you why, but that guy just drove me crazy. I couldn't stand that he wouldn't break. I hated his shit-eating grin. Blood on his teeth and a shit-eating grin."

"Maybe he reminded you of yourself a little bit."

"Maybe."

A car approached our bench, a dark colored sedan that slowed. I turned to look, but the Kid snapped at me. "Eyes forward."

I turned back, and we waited. I watched the Kid, and his eyes followed the sedan.

"Be ready to bolt," he said. "It's stopping."

I heard a car door open, and then a high-pitched, girlish voice reached us.

"I'll call for a ride later," it said.

The Kid's posture relaxed. He let out a deep breath while the car drove off.

"It's nothing," he said. "Just some parent dropping

off their bimbo daughter."

I sank back against the bench, letting the tension ease out of my shoulders and back. "Jesus," I said. "I thought that was it."

"It's all right." The Kid reached down and took another sip from his drink. He rattled the ice and drank some more. "But we should be moving on soon. I don't like being a sitting duck." He threw the cup toward a garbage can, missing it entirely. "Anyway, we couldn't break this guy. And he knew it. He liked to taunt us. Some guys just wanted to kill him, beat him to death. But what good would that do? He'd win, basically. I think he wanted to die. Why give into him that way?

"So one night we pulled him out of his cell. Some guys just wanted to beat on him, I guess. They did that when they were bored. They'd get this guy out of his cell and use him as a human punching bag. I was just watching the whole thing. Shit, I was bored, too. Then I had to take a shit, so I left. But while I was in the bathroom I had an idea. If he liked the sex so much, maybe he'd like something up his ass that he'd never had up there before, you know?"

I squirmed on the bench, involuntarily.

"I brought the plunger back with me. I'm sure you can imagine where this is going, but let's just say it took four guys to hold him down and strip off his pants. That was the first time I saw fear in that boy's eyes. And I mean real fear, the kind I only ever saw on the battlefield. Terror. Since it was my idea, they let me do the honors. I forced that thing up inside that boy. I could feel the resistance, but I forced it anyway, tearing skin and intestines and whatever got in the way. And he screamed and screamed and screamed until he lost his voice. And let me tell you, Jett, I loved every minute of it. I loved it. I loved breaking that guy down and reducing him to tears.

168

That was real power."

The Kid's story not only caused me to squirm, but a gnawing knot of sickness grew in my gut. I wanted to tell him to stop but didn't.

"He bled. A lot. The plunger ruptured something inside of him, the intestinal wall…I don't know. Internal injuries. He died during the night, sometime after we put him back in his cell. Of course, the brass panicked. They called us all onto the carpet, got our stories, and then set about covering it all up. As long as the story never got out, as long as the press didn't get a hold of it, and we didn't squeal, no charges would be filed, and we could stay in the service. They rotated us all out, of course. And wouldn't you know it, we all ended up in the areas with the most intense fighting. I lost my leg three weeks later. Two of the other guys were killed. I don't know what happened to the others, but one of them must have squealed. Or the press got a hold of it somehow. I guess it doesn't really matter, does it? What's done is done.

"Besides, I always knew somebody would spill it. I knew we'd end up getting caught. Have you ever met someone who could keep a secret? I mean really keep one?"

"There aren't many."

"None. There's not one." He wiped his nose with his finger. "I guess that's why I live the way I do. When I came back and got this job, I figured my time was short. Maybe I should have died on the field, so I've sort of lived in a hurry, figuring the curtain's due to drop at any time."

We faced west, and the sun had moved past its apex, its rays slanting across the city.

"I'm not sure I wanted to hear all of that," I said. "But thanks for telling me."

"I'm not done yet," he said.

"There's more?"

"Not much. But it's important. I want you to understand that I did what I thought I had to do to survive. The rules were different over there, and I thought I was doing the right thing. But more than anything, it was about survival, pure and simple."

"I see."

"You should. Because you and I were not that different. When you left your partner behind in that alley, you were doing what you thought you had to do to survive. And so was I. And when you left your wife and kid behind today, same thing. It's all about choices, Chief. The choices we make, the consequences we have to live with. And if we go in there tonight and die…"

I finished his thought. "That's a choice, too."

He didn't say anything else. He was up off the bench and heading for the car.

TWENTY-THREE

O'Neill had left behind maps that showed the entry points to the city. All of these entry points were guarded by military personnel, but the Kid pointed to one on the far west side of the city, near the river.

"Look at this one," he said, tapping the map. We had no idea where O'Neill had acquired the information, nor what price had been paid for it. He included no notes with the maps. We were left to interpret them on our own. "This is where we should go in tonight."

We were in my car, cruising the west side of town. The park hadn't felt safe, so we had spent the afternoon driving around, moving from place to place, wasting time before we could make our move. The Kid had the maps spread out on his lap, and he studied them while I drove.

"Why there?"

"It's the most isolated. There's the most distance from that checkpoint to the others. If we stir up trouble, it will take awhile for help to arrive."

"And the trouble we might stir up is...?"

"Getting past them," the Kid said. "They're not going to want to let us in. That's why you were smart to take those keys."

171

"You're not serious, are you?"

The Kid broke out in a big grin. "Serious as a heart attack," he said. "We have to go and get that rig."

I wasn't convinced. While I voiced my concerns, the Kid ignored me, studying the maps like he was about to take an exam.

"I think we're fools for doing this," I said. "I think they'll be looking for you there."

The Kid shook his head. "No way."

He left it at that.

"You're sure you want to go back for the rig?" I asked. "You're sure you don't want to go in like this?"

The Kid looked up from his studying. "It was your idea. How do you think they're more likely to let us in there?" he said. "In this car or in a city rig?"

"I don't think they'll let us in at all."

"Me either," he said. "But we have a better shot with the rig."

*   *   *

We waited until dusk and headed for the shed. We approached from the east, cutting the lights on my car when we came in sight of the fenced lot. The crusher, a large, black form in the twilight, heaved and pounded, continuing its never ending onslaught against the cars we collected. A smaller crew worked the crusher at night, and the drivers would be long gone to their scattered lives.

"See anything?" I said. "Any trouble?"

"No. But it's too dark anyway. I say we drive in and take the damn thing. Just walk in there like you belong."

"How will I get into the garage?"

"Use your ID card. Swipe it and go in."

"You don't think they've deactivated it already?" I

said.

"There's a chance. But does the city ever do anything on time?"

"They're pretty efficient about firing people."

The Kid took this nonchalantly.

"Then we go to plan B," he said.

"And what's that?"

"I'll come up with something while you're in there."

So I went for it. I drove my car into the parking lot, through the still open gate, and pulled in next to the employee entrance to the garage. The building looked quiet. Only a few lights burned, allowing the guys who worked the night shift on the crusher access to the break room and vending machines.

My heart thumped like a bass drum. I hesitated, my hands still on the wheel.

"You're on, Chief. Take the plunge."

"If there's any trouble," I said, "you can—"

"Don't worry. I'll save my own skin first." He smiled. "If I see trouble, I'll lay on the horn three times in a row. That's your sign to haul ass."

I willed myself out of the car. I looked around the lot and saw nothing.

I stepped over to the door and brought out my magnetic swipe ID. I really didn't believe it would work, but when I ran it through, the green light appeared and the lock disengaged.

I grabbed the handle and pulled it open, giving the thumbs-up to the Kid. I eased inside the large, open space of the garage.

All was silent. Nothing moved or stirred. Before me, an easy path opened to the trucks. I moved across the concrete floor, my echoing footfalls the only sound, until I reached our number one rig. It looked fit and sound, ready to go.

I went over to the switch that opened the garage bay door and flipped it. The door rumbled to life, rising and creaking above my head. Back at the truck, keys in hand, I had opened the door and took a step onto the running board when someone called my name.

I spun. I thought it was the Kid. But why would he come in?

"Over here, Jett."

I heard the footsteps approaching, then saw the figure emerge from across the room. "Bobby," I said. "What are you doing here so late?"

"I was going to ask you the same thing," he said. He came toward me and stopped, crossing his arms across his big chest. "I was going to ask what you were doing here at all. I understand you quit today."

"More or less," I said.

The last time we had talked, Bobby pushed me up against a wall. Residual hostility seemed to linger in the air between us like a bad odor. My heart rate, which had eased once I had the garage door open, picked up again, fueled by adrenaline which was telling my body it might have to fight.

"So what gives?" he said. "Are you planning on stealing that rig?"

I looked behind me at the rig in question then turned to face Bobby again. "Did Ned have a meeting with you all today?"

"He did."

"And he came clean about the City People?"

Bobby shook his head. "What do you mean by that?" he said. "He told us that you had quit, and McGruder was still out, so we were all going to have to pick up the pace if we wanted to make our quotas. That's what I'm doing here so late. I stayed out until almost dark tonight."

"They're lying to you."

"What are you talking about? You sound half nuts."

"About the City People. They're not what they seem to be. Nothing is what it seems to be."

I told him what the Kid and I had seen and what we had learned from O'Neill. I told him about the traps, and the City People smuggling themselves out in the trunks of the cars we hauled.

He tilted his head and considered me with one eye, like a cautious bird. He didn't say anything.

"I found all this out over the last few days and brought it to Ned. Me and my partner. Ned knew all along. They've been using us, Bobby."

His face remained suspicious, but his posture relaxed. He uncrossed his arms. "Bullshit," he said, but his heart wasn't in it.

"I've seen it, Bobby. I've seen them up close. You know that."

My reference to Vince's death must have registered. He turned his body ninety degrees to mine and slumped back against the side of the rig. While he gathered his thoughts, my mind turned to the Kid, who was sitting outside in my car, probably wondering what was happening to me.

"Could you hold on just a second, Bobby?" I said.

He didn't give any indication that he had heard me, so I walked back outside to the car and told the Kid to give me a few more minutes.

"I was just about to come in after you, Chief," he said. "Search and rescue."

"Sit tight. Everything's okay."

"Whatever you're doing in there, hurry it up. I'm not good at waiting."

When I returned to the rig, Bobby had taken a seat on the running board. A cigarette burned in his hand, the smoke curling up toward the fluorescent lights overhead. He didn't look up when he spoke. "I knew something was going on," he said. "I heard some of those same things. We all did. I just convinced myself it was nothing, that the City People would be dying out soon enough and the world would return back to the way it always was."

"Me too."

"What woke you up?" He looked up at me now, squinting through the smoke from his cigarette. "Was it Vince dying?"

"Partially. To be honest, my partner helped a lot. It's tough to stay asleep with him around."

Bobby took a last, long drag before flipping the butt to the floor, and then ground it under his work boot. His gestures conveyed disgust. "I guess that's worth something, isn't it?"

"You were right about him, Bobby. He is crazy." I spoke in a low voice, even though I doubted the Kid could hear me. "And he did stuff in the war...stuff that shouldn't be talked about."

"Don't worry, people *are* talking about it. They were here looking for him today and asking questions."

"I wouldn't be here if it weren't for him. I wouldn't be about to do what I'm going to do."

Bobby fished in his pocket and brought out his pack of cigarettes and lighter. "I know what you're going to do," he said, sticking the cigarette in his mouth and striking the lighter with the smooth, fluid motions of a long-term smoker. "I'd like to think I'd do the same thing if I were in your shoes. I'm not sure if I could, though. It takes some mixture of crazy, stupid and brave that I don't think I have." He pushed himself up off the rig. "You're a good man, Jett. I believe your story, and I believe that you came here to warn us off."

He held his hand out to me, and we shook.

"Thanks, Bobby."

"Thank you." He held on to my hand, his grip as firm as a vice. "And I'm going to come with you to get Vince back."

"No." I released his hand. "No. You don't have to do that."

"I can't let you go alone."

"I'm not. I've got the Kid with me."

Bobby couldn't conceal his disapproval of that plan. "That's what I'm afraid of," he said. "I'm not sure I trust you out there with just him watching your back."

"It's okay," I said. "I cast my lot with him a long time ago. There's no going back on that."

"Loyalty's a bitch sometimes."

"Yes, she is. Besides, you need to stay here and warn the other drivers. If Ned's fat ass isn't going to do it, you need to. Somebody has to sound the alarm. I get the feeling things might be ready to start flying apart. Not just here, but everywhere."

"That sounds about right."

And then there was nothing more to say to each other. We shook hands one more time then I pointed to the rig. "I'm going to take this, okay? You don't mind."

"I don't. It seems like we might be done with this work for awhile."

Bobby stepped back while I climbed in and started the rig. When I dropped it into gear, he waved and called out. "Good luck, Jett. I hope you find what you're looking for."

I waved back, through the open driver's window. "I hope we all do," I said.

TWENTY-FOUR

By the time I rumbled around and met the Kid, he was wound up like a top. He followed me out into the street, driving my car, and we parked it on a side street a few blocks away. I wondered if I'd ever lay eyes on it again, but, still, it held me to this world. My fears and anxieties lessened just a bit knowing that the car waited for my return.

The Kid climbed into the cab. Before he had the door shut, his mouth started running. "I can't believe you left me sitting out there like that," he said. "I'm the one they're after, and you leave me hanging outside the door like a dog tied to a post."

"I was talking to Bobby."

"Bobby? Mister Clean Jeans? What the fuck did he want?"

"He wanted to come with us," I said.

"Bullshit. We don't need his help."

"That's what I told him."

"Damn straight. Why the fuck are just sitting here?"

We idled on the side street where we left the car, the diesel engine rumbling like a hungry beast. In the dark, the green dashboard lights illuminated the Kid's face from below, giving him an otherworldly appearance.

"I don't know, Kid. I guess there's nothing left to wait for."

He brought the map out of the pocket of his coveralls. "Then I've got one thing left to say. Right on Main, south on Eighth, don't stop until you see the checkpoint."

*   *   *

We didn't have a clearly defined plan on how to get past the checkpoint.

We had cooked up several options, none of which sounded likely to succeed.

The Kid favored running it. He thought we should just start from a distance, build up a head of steam in the big rig and blast our way through the barricade. By the time they figured out what was going on, we'd be way past, leaving the soldiers in a scramble to catch up with us.

I hoped to hold this option in reserve.

I wanted to roll up to the checkpoint in the rig and pass ourselves off as city employees on a routine mission. Assuming word hadn't circulated about us, we might get waved through. If we didn't get waved through...we could try another checkpoint. Or try the Kid's method, since desperation was the mother of reckless invention.

We spotted the checkpoint several blocks ahead of us. They turned giant floodlights on at night, and the area around the checkpoint resembled an illuminated athletic field, the bright lights casting an inverted cone of whiteness over the halftracks and jeeps.

The Kid placed his hand on my arm.

"Are you going to run it, Chief?" he said.

"Only if I have to. I'm going to try to talk our way

through first."

The Kid let out a disgusted snort.

"The meek don't inherit a damn thing," he said. "I knew I should have driven."

"Just let me do the talking," I said.

"That's fine. But look." He reached inside his coveralls and brought out a sleek, black pistol. It gleamed in the dashboard light like a strange, obsidian totem. "If your talking doesn't work and you don't run that barricade hard and fast enough, this becomes our plan B."

I gripped the wheel hard and guided us forward.

*   *   *

The sentry who held up his hand and stopped us looked surprisingly young. He wore sergeant's stripes on his sleeve and stood out from his comrades simply by looking fresh-faced and eager. I took his youth to be a bad sign. I figured that some world-weary veteran would be much more likely to wave us through without examining our story.

The young guy looked in the driver's side window at us. The generator that fired the floodlights rumbled in the background, and the soldier spoke up to be heard. "Late night, gentlemen?"

"You know how it is. We have to work for a living."

The sergeant nodded. "I can't let you in," he said. "We don't have any orders for you people to go in tonight. And, as you know, we don't go to the bathroom without orders around here."

He seemed amiable enough on the surface, but his words carried an edge of authority. It reminded me of talking to a cop. No matter what they said, it sounded intimidating. This effect may have been aided by the rifle hanging over his shoulder.

"Are you sure, sergeant?" I said. "I thought this was cleared."

I was tap dancing. I didn't need to look over at the Kid. I felt him. He gave off heat like a furnace and ticked like a time bomb.

The sergeant narrowed his eyes at me and leaned closer. "What exactly are you boys fixing to do? Are you getting into some kind of trouble?"

The Kid stirred next to me. He made a low rumbling sound in his throat. I held my hand out, hoping to calm him.

"No, sir. It's just work. If you could just go and double check your orders, maybe you'll see it."

He held his squinted gaze on me long enough to dry all the saliva in my mouth. But I returned the stare and simply waited until the sergeant nodded.

"You all sit tight," he said. "Let me check."

He walked off to another vehicle, a half-track, where a man in a helmet with a lieutenant's bar sat. The sergeant started talking and pointed back at us.

"Now," the Kid said. "Gun it."

"No."

"Now."

He slipped his foot over to my side of the cabin and tried to press the accelerator.

"Kid!" My foot slipped off the brake and then right back on while I tried to stop him. The rig lurched then stopped.

The army guys all looked our way, caution on their faces. The sergeant came back over to us. "You boys okay?"

"Fine, fine. My foot slipped."

He looked at me, then at the Kid. His eyes were like lasers. "Maybe you two should step out of the vehicle for a moment."

"Look, Sergeant—"

"Don't you have anything better to do than break the balls of a couple of working guys?" the Kid said. "I had my fill of sergeant's bullshit when I was in. Fuck you."

"Kid—"

"Excuse me?" The sergeant reached for my door handle. "You will exit this vehicle. Both of you."

"Sergeant Olding!"

The voice cut through the air with a parental authority. We all froze.

The lieutenant from the half-track, a man close to sixty, ambled over toward the rig, his hand resting on his sidearm. His gut protruded slightly and hung over his belt buckle, but a palpable sense of power emanated from him. "Sergeant Olding, step away from that vehicle." The sergeant stepped back. "Go help Corporal Baines with the nightly report."

Sergeant Olding hesitated, training those laser eyes on the Kid, like a dog separated from a juicy steak. "Yes, sir," he said and turned to go, his posture ramrod straight beneath the floodlights.

The Lieutenant watched Olding go, his hand still resting on the sidearm. His name, Paulman, was stitched onto the breast pocket of his uniform jacket, and when Olding was out of earshot, he turned back to us. "He's young, a little bullheaded." Paulman chuckled. "Me, I'm just bullheaded."

The words came out of my mouth without thinking. "Yes, sir," I said.

Lieutenant Paulman nodded. "A little chilly tonight," he said. "I'm ready for spring, myself." He didn't look cold. His hands were bare, his jacket lightweight. "So you boys think you want to go into the city tonight, is that it?"

"Yes, sir. We're behind in our quotas, and we need to get caught up."

One corner of Paulman's mouth rose, the beginnings of a smile. "You know what we call that where I come from? A thin tissue of horseshit."

The Kid stirred next to me. I expected him to make another lunge for the gas, but he didn't.

"Well, sir..."

"Don't sir me, boy. You're not military. I can tell." He looked over at the Kid. "This one's military. I can tell by the crazed look in his eye. Crazier than a shithouse rat from what I can see."

"Yes, sir," the Kid said and snapped off a sharp salute.

"But not you," Paulman said to me. "You don't have that look about you. The five mile stare, the aura of shit-eating desperation."

I swallowed hard. I shifted my foot a little on the brake.

"Now tell me, what exactly are you boys hoping to go in there for? You're not looking to hunt for City People, are you? Believe it or not, we get a number of yokels coming down here trying to do that. Some of them even get through. They bring their hunting gear, their bows and arrows, and they think they're going to have a big time in the city."

I could tell that Paulman wanted me to ask, so I did. "What happens to them?"

"They don't come back." His smile opened wide, revealing stumpy, yellow teeth. "We did get a call from your supervisor, just a few minutes ago, telling us that a crew was going to be out, working late, and to let them through if they showed up at one of our checkpoints. I know that neither one of you ass-bags made the call because it did come from your headquarters, and I figure you two were driving here when that call was made."

Bobby, I thought. "You're right," I said. "We didn't make that call."

"That's what I said, isn't it? So, you know what I'm going to do? I'm going to let you on through. Hell, if you want to go in there and play Russian Roulette, be my guest. But can I give you a piece of advice first, advice from a man who's been in combat and seen a thing or two in the city?"

I nodded, and so did the Kid.

Paulman's features softened. His eyes looked kinder, almost fatherly. "Turn around and go back," he said. "Go back to your wives or your girlfriends or whatever you have. Whatever's in there isn't worth finding. And it sure isn't worth dying for."

A gust of wind kicked up and blew through our cab. It caused a shiver to run up my arms, but Paulman didn't move. He stayed locked in place, his gaze focused on my face.

"Thanks for the advice, Lieutenant," I said. "But we respectfully disagree."

"I figured you might." He straightened up and called something to the other men. They scrambled into place and opened the gate before us, revealing our passage into the city. "But you're on your own from here on out. If you get into trouble you can't get out of, we're not coming in to help."

"I understand," I said.

Paulman stepped back and waved us through. "I hope you do," he said. "I surely hope you do."

TWENTY-FIVE

Our entry point still left us three miles from the stadium. We would take Eighth Street for about a mile then veer off to the right on Central Boulevard, the main thoroughfare that ran along the front of the stadium.

I cruised at a slow, steady rate, moving my head from side to side to check for trouble. The streetlights on either side still burned, which meant the power grid hadn't been wiped out. If the City People ever did go away, we'd be able to move back in and start up right where we left off before. The only question was: Would anybody want to?

"Must've been Bobby who made that call," the Kid said. "Nice move."

I nodded.

The buildings down there looked better than the ones at the north end of the city where we usually worked. We were in the part of the city where the lawyers and business people worked, the ones who made the money and kept it flowing around. They had left long ago, taking their theatres and martini bars and Indian restaurants with them, out to the suburbs and the gated communities. Like the north end of the city, mid-town and downtown were just shells, like brittle cornstalks left to dangle and shiver in the wind. Except these buildings wouldn't just up and blow away. They'd decay and decline, but not in any great hurry, and that made the place look even sadder and more desolate, an oversized monument to the loss of the city we all once called home.

The Kid actually seemed more relaxed now that we were inside the barricades and moving forward. He started whistling a song I didn't recognize, and he gaped out the window like a wide-eyed tourist.

"Are you happy to be free of everybody's strings?" I said.

He didn't look at me when he answered. "You think we're free?"

"Didn't we just cross the last barrier?" I said. "You heard the Lieutenant—we're in here on our own."

We made the turn onto Central Boulevard. I wasn't certain, because its light towers weren't lit, but I thought I could make out the top of the stadium in the distance.

"So you're not doing this for anybody but yourself?" he said.

"I'm doing it for a lot of people. Vince. Marie. Even Nicole and Sophie, in a way."

The Kid slumped back against his seat. "Then you see my point," he said. "Nobody ever does anything without answering to somebody."

"I thought you didn't want to have anyone to report to."

"I try." He patted his coveralls where I knew the gun was tucked. "But say you cut all the strings and leave the bosses behind. Then what do you answer to?"

"You've got me. I don't know."

I tried to ignore his philosophical ramblings and keep my attention fixed on the road and the task at hand. But the Kid had a way of redirecting me, and I listened to his answer with more curiosity than I wanted to admit.

"Fate," he said. "The big wheel in the sky. You and me ending up partners. Maybe that's fate. Me getting my leg blown off. Who knows? Maybe fate. And what we're about to do tonight — or at least try to do tonight — it sure has the odor of fate about it. Like something we're meant to do, something we have to do. Doesn't it, Jett?"

I told him I agreed, but then we stopped talking. We rounded a bend, and the stadium came into view.

*   *   *

The Kid reached back into his pocket and brought out another map, something else we had found on O'Neill's disc.

"When we get to the stadium, take Wolves Way. It runs up the west side of the stadium to where O'Neill's map says to go in."

The Kid's words barely registered with me. Instead, I focused on the stadium, a four-story, brick and glass structure that at one time housed our city's professional baseball team. Taxpayer money had paid for it, and when it was brand-new, some twenty years earlier, it stood as the high water mark of our civic pride and can-do spirit. The stadium rose at a time when the future of the downtown looked to be in jeopardy, and the hope at the time, among civic leaders and citizens alike, was for the new stadium to kick off a renaissance for the inner city. All these years later, those dreams had crashed, and the darkened stadium sat empty, inhabited only by the City People, a constant reminder of this unmet goal.

"I don't remember," I said. "Did you used to come down here when you were young and go to ballgames?"

"I'm not much for team sports," the Kid said.

"I came down here with Vince the year before the

stadium closed," I said. "Things were pretty bad down here already. It felt like you were taking your life in your hands just coming to a game, and that was before all of this happened. It seems like a million years ago."

"Look there."

The Kid pointed to our left, to the north side of the street.

Three figures—and they had to be City People—moved along the sidewalk and then slipped into an alley between two buildings.

"There," I said.

On the other side of the street, there were three more. When they spotted us, they didn't run or turn away. They just stared, like we were a rare and exotic creature, previously believed to be extinct. The Kid reached for his gun.

"No," I said.

"Why not?"

"We're not here for that."

"Collateral damage, remember?"

"They're not trying to stop us."

"That's what I'm afraid of," he said, but he left the gun alone. "They already showed they know to run an ambush. We might be driving right into one now."

His words chilled me. Even though I had already thought of the possibility on my own, hearing the Kid give voice to the same fear made it all the more real. Despite O'Neill's guidance from beyond the grave, we had no real notion of what we were stepping into.

We turned onto Wolves Way, the two-lane road that gave access to the stadium and its parking garages. The road before us was empty, not a vehicle or City Person in sight. The stadium's superstructure loomed over us on the left, and looking up at the top gave me a vertiginous sensation in my head and gut, one all out of proportion to the building's actual size. But it was our mission which dizzied me.

"Around back, there's an entrance," the Kid said. "It used to be where the players went in. According to O'Neill it should be relatively clear. We can get in that way and start looking."

"I hope he's right."

"If he isn't, it's going to be a real quick night."

The stadium stretched for several blocks, and at the end, we found a ramp that led down to a lower level at the back. We still encountered no resistance or obstacle, and rather than settling my mind, this increased my unease.

At the bottom of the ramp, we entered a parking garage beneath the stadium. Our headlights illuminated a door with a sign that read: PLAYERS AND TEAM PERSONNEL ONLY.

"This is it," the Kid said. "That's the door."

I eased the rig to a stop.

Many of the lights anchored in the ceiling of the garage were burned out or broken, so visibility was spotty. Water dripped from a broken pipe near us and gathered in a large puddle on the floor. I didn't like sitting in the dark that way, not being able to see what might or might not be around us and watching our movements. Apparently, the Kid didn't either.

"Let's go," he said.

He reached down and brought out our weapons of choice, the bat and the tire iron. I shut the rig down and turned off the lights, which meant we had to travel the distance from the cabin to the door—which was supposed to be unlocked, according to O'Neill's notes— in the murky half-darkness. Just as I would gather a large breath before jumping into a deep pool of water, I inhaled and pushed the door open. The Kid opened his door and stepped out.

We moved quickly, our footfalls echoing through the large open space. I reached the door ahead of the Kid and pulled on the handle. At first, it didn't move, but then I gave it a harder yank, and it slipped open. The Kid went in, and I followed and let the door shut behind us.

We had entered a short hallway. Fluorescent lights overhead still burned, reflecting off the cinderblock walls which had been painted bright blue, one of the team colors of the Wolves. At the end of the hall was a set of double doors and we made for those.

"Through there," the Kid whispered.

At the double doors, we paused. I tightened my grip on the bat, and the Kid did the same with the tire iron. He nodded at me then pushed through the door like a cop serving a felony warrant. I went right behind him, but there was nothing to see. We were in another hallway, one that ran crossways to the first. The Kid jerked his head to the right, indicating the direction we should go, so again, I followed.

This hallway smelled mildewy and damp, and beneath everything, a faint odor of rotten garbage hovered, a testament to the stadium's neglect and disuse. Without pausing to say anything to me, the Kid opened another door, and only when I made it there myself did I see that the sign there read: Wolves' Clubhouse.

Again, we stood in half-light. Lockers covered every inch of available wall space, and the royal blue carpet beneath our feet squished with every step. There had obviously been a leak. The clubhouse felt stuffier than the hallway, more closed off and isolated, and the smell of human urine burned my nose.

"What do you think?" the Kid said.

"Maybe O'Neill was wrong. Maybe no one's here, or else they moved on."

"No way. They're here. Probably upstairs. The map

190

shows a tunnel that goes from here out to the field, and an escalator that goes up to the next levels. We need to head that way."

"Let's keep alert."

"Of course."

But the Kid didn't move. He stood rooted to his spot in the center of the clubhouse, taking in the spare and abandoned surroundings. "It's weird, isn't it?" he said.

"You're just noticing that."

"I mean this room. At one time, think of the guys who hung out in here. All their money, all their fame. And now look at the place. It's a litter box for City People."

"I would have given anything to be in here when the Wolves played here. It would have been like entering the Vatican."

"Look on my works ye mighty and despair," the Kid said.

"What's that all about?"

"It's from a poem. 'Ozymandias.' It means everything passes and fades away. Even the mightiest and the strongest. I read it in high school, too."

"Did he build a wooden horse?"

"No. Just a big statue of himself that turned to dust. Come on. Let's go."

TWENTY-SIX

We walked up a broken escalator to the next level of the stadium. It let us out on the concourse amid the closed concession stands and empty souvenir kiosks. We were on the plaza level, behind the lower level of seats, just behind first base. The light was dimmer there. Some ambient light spilled in from the city, but the stadium bowl itself was dark, and if there had been a game underway on the field, we couldn't have seen it.

We hesitated and listened. Nothing greeted us but the silence. I had been in that place when fifty thousand people cheered as one, but the emptiness of that big stadium roared in my ears even louder.

"Home plate, Chief," the Kid said. "Let's head for home."

We moved to the left.

Our shoes scraped cautiously over the concrete, the Kid slightly ahead of me. I held the bat in my hand, of course, my grip so tight my knuckles hurt. How I wished I could simply go down on the field and, rather than living out this nightmare, live out instead my childhood dream of playing baseball on the same ground my heroes walked. How nice it would be to run the film of the past few weeks and months and years in reverse, and watch the Kid go away and Vince return to life, and see the city itself return to what it once had been when the world was younger and better.

Then something scuttled across our path about fifty feet ahead of us.

We stopped.

"Did you see that?" the Kid said.

"I heard it."

"Someone ran into that room up there."

The door squeaked shut. I looked up.

"It's the men's room," I said.

"It looked like a little kid, I swear. Come on."

When we reached the door, the Kid tilted his head forward, listening. "I don't hear anything in there." He looked back at me. "I'm going in there. What if your partner's in there?" He reached into his coveralls and drew out the gun. "Take this. Stand guard."

"No." I pushed the gun back toward him. "I'll go."

"You sure, Chief?"

"Remember our deal? When we find Vince..."

"I remember. Don't you trust me?"

"You can stand guard," I said.

The Kid reached for the door handle and looked at me.

"I'm ready," I said.

"There's light in there," he said, pointing to the crack of brightness that leaked out the bottom of the door. "Look fast. If there's trouble, bolt."

"I will."

He pulled the door open.

I took three quick steps in and turned my body for a view of the entire room. It was bright, blindingly bright after the murk of the concourse. Every light burned and reflected off the white tile walls and floor.

My eyes swept the room. Nothing. No one.

"Hello," I said, and my voice bounced off the walls and came back at me.

The stalls at the far end of the room provided the only cover. I took a few steps that way, bending down a little so that I could look for feet. The fluorescent bulbs above the mirrors buzzed a steady drone of white noise.

I was halfway across the room when I saw a shoe. Then another.

I stopped.

They belonged to a child. Dirty and scuffed sneakers.

"Hey," I said, trying to make my voice as soft and non-threatening as possible. "You can come out."

The child didn't move.

Then I caught a glimpse of myself in the mirrors. A grown man, tired and haggard, wearing an iron gray jumpsuit and holding a baseball bat. What kind of figure did I cut? Would a child, any child, trust me? Did I want this child to think I was a lunatic?

I went over and leaned the bat against the wall between the sinks. I moved closer to the stalls and spoke again.

"It's okay. You can come out. I'm just looking for someone, a friend of mine. I thought maybe you had seen him."

I waited. I decided that if the child didn't want to come out and talk to me, I would just turn around and go. I was about to do so when the child took a tentative step forward. Then another. The lock on the stall door rattled — he had locked himself in there to get away from me — and then the door swung inward.

He was a boy, about eight years old. In all respects he looked like an average child. Dirty blonde hair, a tiny, slightly bulbous nose. He had a certain sallowness of the skin, accentuated by the sickly fluorescent lights, and it was the only sign of illness or disease on his body. He didn't appear as gray and shambling as the other City People I had seen, the ones who looked as though they were in some kind of waking vegetative state.

The boy hung close to the stall door and looked at me with suspicious eyes.

"Hi," I said.

It felt odd trying to make small talk with a child who might very well have wished to destroy me, but I tried to cling to O'Neill's words and use them as a life preserver. These people weren't what we'd been told they were. Don't fall for the propaganda, I reminded myself.

So I forged ahead. "Have you seen a man dressed like me? A man wearing clothes like these?" I tugged on my coverall.

The boy continued to stare at me, but I thought I saw something cross his face, some hint of recognition or understanding.

"Have you seen a man like that?"

Almost imperceptibly, the boy nodded.

"You have?"

He nodded again, this time with more vigor.

"Is he here? Is he...alive?"

The boy looked a little scared, which made my heart jump, but then he nodded again.

Before I rejoiced, the thought crossed my mind that this child might have a different definition of "alive" than I did. Did he mean as alive as himself, or as alive as the other City People, the ones I had seen while working? Could I even trust this child at all? But I shuffled those questions aside. I had to take what I could get.

The boy studied me just as the City People on the road outside had studied me, as if I were a curiosity in a zoo. No doubt his head had been filled with some manner of propaganda, some warning against those of us who came from the outside. But rather than making me more nervous or edgy, this thought calmed me and made me wish that I could disavow him of those notions. My thoughts turned to my own Sophie, not even a year old and already on the brink of a life without her father. The world really didn't need anyone else growing up confused and lost, wishing for direction that never came.

I looked over at my bat and decided to leave it there. I held out my hand to the child. "Can you show me where my friend is?" I said. "Can you take me to him?"

The boy pulled back, nestling himself against the dirty stall door.

"It's okay," I said again, my hand still out between us. "Just take me to him. Please?"

The boy extended his hand. But he didn't want to take mine. Instead, his index finger pointed toward me. "You're a bad man," he said.

His words hit me like a slap. "No. I'm not a bad man."

"You're a killer."

His words carried an anger and invective that I hadn't imagined a child so young could possess. I opened my mouth to respond, but words didn't form. The boy backed away, a look of sheer terror spreading across his face.

"No," I said. "Not me."

The Kid's gun fired on the concourse, three shots in quick succession.

I spun toward the sound.

The gun fired two more times.

"Jett!" he shouted. "We've got a problem!"

TWENTY-SEVEN

On the concourse, I found the Kid surrounded by a semi-circle of at least a dozen City People. Several of them lay dead in the open space between us and them, the result of the Kid's gunshots.

The Kid held the gun in one hand, the tire iron in the other. Everything froze in a moment of stasis. The City People appeared to be waiting to see what we would do. We were cut off and would have to fight our way out.

"Where's your bat?"

"Fuck. I left it inside."

"Forget it." He handed me the tire iron. "We're pretty well fucked anyway."

"Why don't they rush?"

The crowd of City People—mostly young, mostly men—watched, occasionally emitting low grunts.

"They're smart. O'Neill was right. They're waiting for us to make a move. They've got the number advantage."

"That boy in there talks," I said. "He can talk."

"They were smart enough to trick us, to ambush us. What do you expect?"

Then, from the far right of the semi-circle, one of the

City People broke away and charged us. The Kid fired twice, and the man fell dead at his feet.

The grunting grew in volume, and then, as if some unspoken signal had been transmitted among them, they all moved toward us.

"Aim for the head," the Kid said, "and swing for the fences."

I swung and connected with the head of the one closest to me. He stumbled back and went down. Another approached, and I swung again. This time, the City Person ducked away, and I fell off balance.

The Kid's gun fired rapidly, a succession of echoing, concussive pops.

I regained my balance.

Another one of them, a woman about my age, approached me from the left. I hit her in the face, knocking her back. The Kid shot at her, hitting her in the chest.

They kept coming, and I kept swinging.

The man I had swung at and missed came back at me. I tried for him again, and this time, he grabbed my wrist, stopping my downward motion. Another one grabbed my left wrist. The tire iron fell to the floor.

They started to drag me down.

Their hands clawed at my hair, my clothes.

"Kid!" I yelled.

His fired two more times, then the gun made a sickening *click-click-click*.

Empty.

*   *   *

Through the tangle of City People around me, I watched as the Kid got pulled down as well. He swung his arms wildly, a windmilling dervish, but he quickly disappeared from my sight in a spray of blood and a deafening scream that quickly turned to indecipherable grunts and then a sickening silence.

They were all over me. I couldn't fight them off. I had the thought, the very clear thought: "This is how my life ends. This is how I go away."

And some part of me welcomed it, welcomed the end. I hoped it would be like going to sleep.

But before the lights went out, I looked up one more time and saw the child from the bathroom standing over me, that tiny index finger extended again, pointing at me, accusing me.

Something clubbed me over the back of the head.

And then I saw no more.

TWENTY-EIGHT

Something held me down. Hands or restraints.

I tried to sit up, but I was groggy. It felt like I'd been asleep for days, and my head hurt like someone had driven a nail into my skull. I was on a bed, in a small room painted royal blue. As I studied the room, I noticed that I wasn't on a typical bed. I was on a medical table, the kind used in doctor's examining rooms. Anatomical posters decorated the walls, showing various types of sports injuries. ACL. MCL. Planter fasciitis. Repetitive motion injuries.

I was in the stadium's training room, bound to the table by thick ropes.

I didn't have the energy to even think about trying to work free. I was exhausted and alone. I let my head fall back against the table, and I slept.

*　　*　　*

Something woke me. Hands slapped at my face, bringing me to sudden consciousness. Still restrained, I looked up into the face of a City Person.

I jerked against the ties that held me to the table, barely moving them.

"Shhhh, Mr. Dormer," she said. "Relax."

I continued to thrash.

"Relax," she said again. "I really don't mean you any harm."

I slowed down. I took a good look at her.

She was black, and not much older than me, but her face displayed the same sallowness as the other City People, which on her tended to appear more like a washed-out grayness. She wore her hair back in a tight bun, and her skirt and blouse, while dingy and frayed, still looked professional, as if the woman had taken great care with her appearance.

"You're one of them," I said.

The woman straightened up, crossing her arms across her chest. She resembled a disapproving schoolteacher. "One of whom, Mr. Dormer? Whom exactly am I one of?"

I gave a last, weak tug against my restraints. "A City Person," I said.

"Your knowledge is so limited," she said, her lips pursed. "I suppose I am what you would call a City Person, but I think that's rather a simplistic way of looking at the world, isn't it? If you'll stop fidgeting, I'd be happy to explain myself to you."

"Where's my partner?"

"The man you came in with?"

I remembered the Kid getting swarmed under. "Yes. Him, too," I said. "Both my partners."

The woman turned her gaze away from mine ever so slightly. "The man you arrived here with didn't survive." She looked at me directly again. "I'm sorry."

My head dropped back against the table. The Kid was gone. It seemed next to impossible to believe that a force that strong, that intense, could be extinguished. His cloak of invincibility had its limits. And now I was left without it.

"What about Vince? I was told he was alive."

The woman nodded. "Yes," she said. "A more complicated case. If you'll relax, I'd be more than happy to tell you all about it, and in the process, perhaps address some of the preconceived notions with which you seem to have arrived."

"Is he alive or dead?" I jerked against the ropes again, straining until the tendons in my neck felt like they would snap.

The woman shook her head. She placed her finger over her lips, telling me to be quiet. "Such a simple question, Mr. Dormer," she said. "So simple and yet so very, very complicated."

When I couldn't strain any more, I fell back. My entire body ached. My throat felt raw.

The woman cleared her throat. "I'm a doctor, Mr. Dormer. Internal medicine. Doctor Renee Blakely." She nodded at me as if we were being introduced at a formal dinner party. "I was a doctor before the attack on our water supply, and I've done my best to continue to work as one after the attack. People here need the kind of care I can provide."

She pulled a stool over and sat down, crossing her legs knee over knee. She wore scuffed and dirty gym shoes that I imagined she wouldn't have been caught dead in under normal circumstances.

"There are a number of misconceptions about what you call the City People. One is that we are all shuffling, shambling, mindless creatures of the night, incapable of speech or thought."

"I guess you've pretty much disproved that one."

She smiled primly. "It's true that some of us do fit that stereotype. The individuals you encountered outside fit that model quite well, and I'm sure the same could be said for those you encountered out in the rest of the city.

But every society needs its soldiers, its workers. Wouldn't you agree?"

"You're saying they're disposable."

"That's a harsh way of putting it, but I suppose we don't really have the time or the inclination to play games with each other. You see, we found out pretty quickly that whatever was put in the drinking water to poison us affected different people different ways. Some became the mutants you have imagined. Some could still speak and retain a type of awareness, but were no longer close to their previous selves. Others, a smaller percentage, became like me."

"Like you?"

She smiled again. "I may seem perfectly normal, according to your definition of that word. But I'm not, I'm afraid to say. Whatever was placed in our water supply — and I admit that I have no idea what it was — has changed me in fundamental ways. True to the stereotype, I can't go out in the direct sunlight. The sun causes irreparable damage to our cells and exposure for any length of time results in death. Intellectually, I don't feel like myself. I may sound articulate and knowledge-able...but I don't feel that way. It's as though my brain is slowing down, unwinding like a clock. In a way, my brain and body are both aging more rapidly than they should, as if the inevitable decay and decline associated with old age have attacked me with twice the force. It's an advanced form of physiological entropy."

"What does this have to do with me? I only came to get Vince."

"Mr. Dormer, I get the feeling I can trust you with those restraints off. If I cut you free, will you behave?"

"As long as no one tries to hurt me."

"No one here wants to hurt you." She opened a drawer behind her and brought out a long, serrated kitchen knife. She brought it toward me and, involuntarily, I flinched. "It's okay," she said. "If we wanted you dead, you'd be long gone."

I tried to relax while she cut the ropes off my body. I flexed my muscles, welcoming the return of normal blood flow to my extremities.

Doctor Blakely tossed the knife back in the drawer and resumed her perch on the stool.

"How long have I been here?"

"A few hours. We're sorry we had to hit you on the head like that, but if you had continued to resist, you might have met the same fate as your partner. I know you have a lot of questions, but our time is getting shorter by the moment."

"Why do you say that? And what about Vince? When do I get to see him?"

She held her index finger up in the air. "Just another moment, please. Your arrival here is something of a big deal for us. We've...taken a number of people from the outside over the past few years. Some came looking for sport, some out of simple curiosity. Others, like your previous partner, came here for work, mostly military men. I'd say, all in all, about twenty-five individuals from your world have made their way into ours and survived the initial encounter. Never once has anyone bothered to pursue them past the gates of the city, and that makes you rather unique in our eyes."

"What do you do with them?"

The bright lights from overhead had begun to hurt my eyes. As if reading my mind, Doctor Blakely switched on a small metal lamp near the sink and turned the overhead lights off, leaving us in a softer, warmer light. "Initially, we'd hoped to ransom them. We'd hoped that the government or the police—somebody—would come looking and make contact with us. They would see that everything down here isn't a lost cause, that people need help. That the city can still be saved. Now. Not twenty years from now. When that didn't work, we decided to study our condition, to try to understand how this illness affects a so-called normal organism. One from the outside."

My brain may still have been foggy. It took a long moment for her words to register. "You experiment on them?" I said. "You infect them on purpose?"

"We felt we were left no choice. We were cut off, and for a long time, many of us were dying. The very notion is loathsome to me, experimenting on human subjects, but we had no other options."

"You could have asked for help. You could have tried to get out."

Anger flashed in Doctor Blakeley's eyes. "Really, Mr. Dormer? Is it that simple? Just ask? Tell me something. If you had heard our voices asking for help, crying for help, would you have listened? Would you have paid us any attention at all had we not taken your partner?"

TWENTY-NINE

"If you're ready to see your partner, Mr. Dormer, I can take you there now," Doctor Blakely said. "But I caution, you probably won't like what you have to see."

I considered her words. I considered everything I had seen and heard over the past month. "I have to see him. It's what I came for. I might not like it, but I have to see it through."

Doctor Blakely nodded. "I'll make the arrangements."

She left the room. I heard the lock turn and engage from her side.

* * *

About half an hour later, Doctor Blakely returned with two men. She led them through the door of the training room. I tensed at the sight of them and backed up.

"It's all right, Mr. Dormer."

The two men were City People, I could tell by looking, but they appeared to be of the higher-functioning variety. When Doctor Blakely gave them orders, they moved.

"We have to bind your hands. Just as a precaution."

My body tensed. The two men were bigger than me. Resistance didn't make much sense. I glanced at Doctor Blakely. She wore a look of disapproval. And she had played straight with me, at least as far as I knew. I just didn't know if I had much fight left in me anyway. I wasn't even sure fighting was worth it anymore.

So I held out my hands.

The two men didn't speak, but they did their work with model efficiency. They pulled the ropes tight, abrading my skin. Then one of them brought out a piece of white cloth and folded it like a blindfold.

"No way." I shook my head. "Bullshit."

The men stopped. They looked to Doctor Blakely.

"That's okay," she said, calm with authority. "I think I'd like Mr. Dormer to see things as they really are here. I think that would be good for him."

The men backed off.

"Ready?" Doctor Blakely said.

I nodded and took a deep breath.

"Ready."

*   *   *

They led me back out onto the concourse, the two men on either side of me and Doctor Blakely taking quick, efficient strides out in front of us. We moved toward home plate again, continuing in the direction that the Kid and I were headed in when we were overwhelmed.

The night air was cool, raising goose bumps on my skin. At first, we didn't pass or see anyone. The concourse was empty, the night quiet. But as we moved along, I started to see shapes standing or sitting on either side of the concrete walkway. I saw, as we drew closer, that they were City People, each and every one of them, and when they saw me, a tension, a negative energy rippled through the crowd.

I stopped. I sensed that they meant to do me harm, and I took a couple of steps back. The two men grabbed me, stopping my motion.

"Enough," Doctor Blakely said.

I wasn't sure who she meant her words for, but some of the murmuring in the crowd ceased. "Come on, Mr. Dormer." She pointed at her watch. "Time is of the essence."

That statement again.

The men's grips on my arm tightened to the point that I knew they were bruising me. My body was rigid, but I didn't have any choice. I relaxed, and the two men shoved me forward. This elicited another round of groans and murmurs from the crowd. They were expressing pleasure at my discomfort.

Doctor Blakely had moved far ahead, disappearing through the crowd and into the darkness. I started walking again, hoping to keep up, hoping she would keep me safe.

I passed through the crowd. Their murmurs increased, the negative energy returned. Someone spit on me, the saliva landing on my neck. A foot-long length of two by four, studded with nails, landed just in front of me. The men guarding me remained calm, almost unaffected. I put my head down. I wished and hoped that they wanted to scare me more than hurt me. Like Doctor Blakely said, if they had wanted to kill me, I wouldn't still be around.

An odor hung in the air, some sort of twin to the anger and resentment seeping out of the crowd. It was the smell of misery. Human beings packed tightly together, generating waste and garbage and body odors, their combined excretions and by-products merging into a rotten emanation that assaulted my senses and gagged me. Even in the open air of the concourse, the odor dominated.

It was a relief to see Doctor Blakely turn to her left ahead and push through a set of double doors. I held my breath until I went through the doors myself and, to my great relief, the air was easier to breathe. She went through another set of doors, and we came out into a short, carpeted hallway, one that wouldn't have been out of place in the headquarters of a bank or insurance company. The two men came through behind me, but stopped and waited at the end of the hallway.

"I'm sorry about the crowd out there," she said, although she didn't sound that distressed. "Like I said, your arrival is a major event here."

"I'm just glad to be out of that smell," I said.

"We've been here a long time, Mr. Dormer. We do our best, but our resources our limited. And getting more limited by the day."

My hands remained tied, my fingers tingling as the blood supply slowed.

Doctor Blakely nodded to a closed door in front of us. "Your original partner is in there," she said. "Vincent Lee. You're welcome to go in and see him. But understand he won't be the way you remember him. He's not the same person who disappeared from your life that day in the city, and you may find that somewhat...*disturbing*." She looked at the closed door, a pensive, almost distant look on her face. "You may spend your time with him as you wish, but I suggest, however, that you don't linger too long. It may become... counterproductive." She nodded to the two men behind me. One of them came forward with the same knife I had seen earlier in the training room. He slit the ropes, freeing me once again. Doctor

Blakely brought out a key and unlocked the door. "When you're finished," she said, "I'll talk to you again."

THIRTY

I turned the knob and pulled the heavy, wooden door open. The room inside was only partially lit. Half the fluorescents in the ceiling were either burned out or turned off. The space appeared to be a conference room, carpeted and large enough to hold a table and chairs, but now it sat empty except for the figure of a man sitting in the corner of the room, his head down between his knees.

I let the heavy door shut behind me.

He wore the same gray coveralls I did. His were dirty and worn, like they'd been dragged through a field of dirt and rocks.

It was Vince.

Unmistakably Vince, my partner, my friend. I recognized his dark hair, the heavy work boots he wore, the way he spread his fingers on top of his knees. I didn't know what to do, so I said his name. "Vince."

He didn't respond.

I took a few steps forward and spoke again. "Vince, it's me, Jett."

He stirred. A slight movement of his head and right hand.

"That's right," I said. "You remember me."

He shook his head as if just waking up. His fingers flexed. It was only when he looked up, and for the first time I saw his face full on, that I understood exactly what Doctor Blakely meant. I recognized the sunken cheeks, the gray, pasty skin and the squinting, lifeless eyes. I recognized them not because they belonged to my partner, Vince, but I recognized that he had become one of them, a City Person through and through.

It appeared as though the effort of raising his head and looking at me had cost him a great deal of energy. His head instantly lolled to his right, dropping down onto his shoulder. His entire body followed suit, and Vince was soon on the floor in some semblance of the fetal position. He looked to be asleep or unconscious, but like the other City People the Kid and I had seen, his eyes remained open.

I fell to my knees in the middle of the room. "Vince," I said, my voice a whisper, "I'm so sorry, man. I'm so sorry for everything." A lone, thick sob blurted out of me like an overwrought hiccup. I bit back on the rest, preventing their release. I pounded my fist against the floor until my hand hurt. "The fucking bastards," I said, "the fucking, goddamn bastards. What did they do to you?"

But I didn't even know who the bastards were anymore. I wanted to exact revenge or justice, but I had no notion of where to start. And I was sure Vince was long gone, just like the world we once knew together.

Until he said my name.

"Jett..." His voice sounded scratchy and thin, like a dirty and dusty record. But it was there. He said my name again. "Jett."

I looked up from my position on the floor. "Vince?"

I couldn't help myself. I was on my feet and made up the distance between us in two long steps and dropped to the floor next to him. I grabbed hold of the front of his coveralls with both hands, lifting his head up, and then put my arms around him and pulled him to me. "I'm here," I said. "I came back for you. You're a fucking beautiful sight, you goddamned jackass."

When I finally let go, I realized I'd been crying. I wiped at my eyes with the backs of my hands. I couldn't remember the last time I had done that. Not even when Sophie was born. Not even when we'd had the memorial for Vince. But right then, in that moment in the empty conference room, all bets were off. I cried like a little girl.

"How did you get in here?" Vince said.

"Oh, man, it's a crazy-ass story. I've seen some shit, boy, and...I've done some shit too. But it got me here. I can tell you all about it, but we've got to get the fuck out of here first." I looked back at the closed door, remembering the scene on the concourse. "This place is going to hell fast, and we need to get you back to Marie and the kids."

Vince's gaze drifted about the room, then fixed on me again. "Marie?" he said. "Is Marie okay?"

"She's okay. The kids are okay. I've been looking out for them a little. I gave them some money. They're fine."

Vince's face showed relief. "Good," he said. "Thank you."

"Come on, we have to get moving." I put my hand on Vince's arm. "It might get ugly. Can you walk? How are you feeling?"

"Not my best."

I nodded. "Okay. We can handle that." I thought about Vince's ability to get us out of trouble in the past, but those days were over. This time it was going to have to be all me. "I'm on this, okay? I made it in here, and I'm going to get us out." I paused. "Do you know what they've done to you?"

This time, something passed across Vince's eyes, the

most visible sign of recognition and intelligence I had seen there since I'd entered the room. "I'm one of them," he said.

"No," I said. "No, you're not."

"Yes. They got me."

"No," I said. "There's different kinds of this thing, some worse than others, some better. You can still talk, you can reason. You're still you, I can see it."

He shook his head, the movement erratic and jerky, like a man with palsy. "Getting worse," he said. "I can feel it."

"No."

"Yes," he said. "I know. I've seen others."

"We'll get you out. We'll get you help somewhere. You used to say we couldn't turn our back on the city, that we all owed it to people down here to help them. What does that mean now?"

His mouth twitched. I thought he was struggling to form words, but then it became obvious that a wry smile was taking shape. "Where is the help?" He looked past me to the empty space of the room. "Who would give it, and when? There's no help, none coming."

I took hold of the front of his coveralls. "I'm not leaving you here again. I'm not telling Marie I came all this way and didn't finish."

"Marie...the kids...they can't see me like this. They can't watch me get worse and fade away..."

I tightened my grip on his clothes. I rose to my feet, planted them against the floor and pulled as hard as I could in an attempt to lift Vince upright. He resisted. He was as big as me and still strong. He still had fight left. He took hold of my arms and pulled against me until he fell back against the wall into his original sitting position, and I fell to the floor in front of him. "Fuck," I said.

I was out of breath, but determined to try again. I

214

reached out for him but he batted my hands away.

"No," he said, his voice strong. It froze me. "Just go. Go while you still can."

"Vince…"

"I told you to go that day in the city. I'm telling you to go now. Go back. Go back and tell them what's really happening here, what's really going on. Tell them."

"I can't leave you here again, Vince. I *can't*."

"I'm already gone."

I continued to shake my head, but I knew he was right. It didn't matter how long or how hard I tried to think of another way, nothing would change that. I pushed myself up off the floor.

I had no idea what fate awaited me outside. I looked around the room, searching for an idea, when I saw something leaning against the wall in the corner. My baseball bat wasn't out of place in the stadium, but it was out of place in that airless, empty room. It was the one I had brought in the rig with me, the one I had used for my work with the Kid. I recognized the red electrical tape wrapped around the handle and the large chip in the barrel.

Someone had retrieved it from the bathroom where I'd left it and brought it to that room. Intuitively I understood the reason why it was there. In this situation, a baseball bat could only be used for one thing.

I had made sure the Kid knew I wanted to be the one to do Vince in. Apparently Doctor Blakely understood the same thing. I couldn't leave Vince that way. He wasn't alive, not in the way he was supposed to be. And not in the way we all—Marie, his kids and me—needed him to be alive.

I picked up the bat. My eyes filled with tears again, but I just wiped them away. I had a job to do. Everything had begun and ended with the job for us. We were the best, and the best always did what they had to do. No matter what.

When I turned and looked at Vince, I saw the recognition in his sad eyes.

"It's okay," he said. "It's okay."

I gripped the bat with both hands. "I'm sorry."

His eyes rolled back to white.

I swung until my work was finished.

THIRTY-ONE

I stepped back out into the hallway. Doctor Blakely waited for me. She stood against the opposite wall, her arms crossed and a stack of papers in her hands. She now wore a white lab coat. I slumped back against the wall across from her.

"I'm sorry, Mr. Dormer. I tried to prepare you, but words are sometimes inadequate."

"You had that bat placed in there," I said.

"I thought you'd like to be there for the end of Mr. Lee's life."

"The life you ended."

She rolled the papers into the shape of a tube and placed them in the pocket of the lab coat. "Like I said, Mr. Dormer, we're all trying to survive."

"Yeah." I felt hollowed out as well, as empty as Vince. "So tell me the truth—how much time do I have?"

Doctor Blakely smiled efficiently, like someone who had been checked in a game of chess. "You're rather perceptive, Mr. Dormer."

"I'm starting to be," I said. "If you've been testing others, you must be testing me. What did you do while I was unconscious? Inject me? Get me to drink some tainted water?"

"Does it matter?" she said. "You're down here with the rest of us no matter what."

"You're right, of course." An idea had started to form in my head. "But I was hoping we could work something out."

Blakeley's eyes widened slightly. "Such as?"

"Let me go back. I promised I'd bring Vince home, or short of his living self, his body. Let me do that. I made promises to people, and for a change, I'd like to keep them."

"And in exchange?"

"I'll tell your story. The *real* story of what's going on in here. I'll find sympathetic ears and tell them what I've seen. The conditions, the despair, the...neglect, I'll—I'll tell them about people like you, the hope."

She leaned back against the wall and slipped her hands into her pockets. She titled her head and considered me. I couldn't blame her for being cautious. She had no reason to trust someone from the outside, someone who had spent the better part of the past month seeking out and destroying the people she was committed to saving. But she also didn't have many choices. Few of us did anymore. "I would ask how I would be able to trust you," she said, "but that seems a silly question."

"You either do or you don't."

"True enough," she said. "Ever since the infection, some of us—those of us like me who maintained our higher functions—have managed to maintain a certain degree of order here. It may not look like it, but we've had enough supplies to get by, and we've managed to keep most of our baser desires in check." She moistened her lips. "But that's changing, Mr. Dormer. I get the sense that we're losing our grip on those things here. Some of our members have already been escaping, finding ways out through the barricades. And more of them are organizing here. We won't stay and rot in what's left of this city forever, much as the powers that be might wish we would. Some day soon there's going to be a reckoning, and no one will be able to do anything to stop it."

"But we can try," I said. "What else is there for us to do?"

She nodded. "Let's go get your keys," she said.

* * *

They loaded Vince's body, wrapped in a sheet, into the back of my rig.

Through the entrance to the garage, I saw the first hint of dawn, rosy light leaking in to the darkness like a path for me to follow. I knew my first stop. Marie's house. After that, it was anybody's guess. I'd have to do something I wasn't very good at. I'd have to reach out. I'd have to ask for help. It wouldn't be easy, but I wouldn't stop. I had thought my mission was complete, but really it had only just begun. And the stakes were even higher now, my sense of purpose inflated.

Doctor Blakeley stood by the side of the cab and spoke to me through the open window. "It's been...fascinating meeting you, Mr. Dormer. I wish you the best."

We shook hands. "Hang on," I told her. "I'll bring help soon as I can."

"Whether you do or don't, I believe you're going to try."

I turned the key, and the rig rumbled to life. The throbbing of its diesel engine filled the garage. "You know, Doc, you never told me how much time I have."

Her forehead wrinkled. "Symptoms typically present within three or four days, seventy-two to ninety-six hours." She checked her watch. "You fell unconscious about five hours ago."

"Good to know."

"But I never answered your question earlier, about whether or not you were infected while you were uncon-scious —"

I held up my hand, stopping her. "It doesn't matter," I said. "Time's short for all of us."

I backed out and headed into the sunlight, my partner, the man for whom I had come that far, riding with me one last time.

And after I fulfilled the promise I made to Marie and Vince, I would be on my own, free to pursue my new promise, the one I had made to Doctor Blakeley and the nameless multitude I didn't even know.

And I was one of them now, a City Person loose in the world, running and fighting.

Hoping.

ABOUT THE AUTHOR

David Jack Bell is an Assistant Professor of Creative Writing at St. Andrews College in Laurinburg, North Carolina. His work has appeared in various journals and anthologies including: *Backwards City Review; Western Humanities Review; The Edge, Tales of Suspense; Shadow Regions;* and *Wicked Karnival Halloween Special Edition.*

You can visit his website at www.davidjackbell.com.

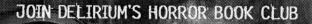

Printed in the United States
119754LV00001B/62/A